Gardner Haines

Love on fire

Gardner Haines

Love on fire

ISBN/EAN: 9783337257217

Printed in Europe, USA, Canada, Australia, Japan

Cover: Foto ©Andreas Hilbeck / pixelio.de

More available books at **www.hansebooks.com**

LOVE ON FIRE,

—OR—

AND BODY WORK.

—BY—

EVANGELIST.

CONTENTS.

CHAPTER.   PAGE,

I. Origin of Good and Evil, - - - 5
II. Man's Relation to God, - - - - 9
III. Fall and Redemption of Man, 14
IV. Salvation by Christ, - - - - - - - 19
V. The New Birth, - - - - - - - - - 24
VI. Trinity of Faith, - - - - - - - - - 27
VII. Faith and Works, - - - - - - - - 33
VIII. Following Jesus, - - - - - - - - 37
IX. Entire Consecration, - - - - - - 41
X. Holy Ghost Fire, - - - - - - - - 46
XI. Purity of Heart, - - - - - - - - - 50
XII. The Extent of Salvation, - - - 54
XIII. Purification, - - - - - - - - - - - 57
XIV. The Anointing Power, - - - - 61
XV. Holiness, - - - - - - - - - - - - - 66
XVI. Preservation, - - - - - - - - - - - 69
XVII. Soul and Body Work, - - - - - 72
XVIII. Sickness an Enemy, - - - - - - 76
XIX. Cause and Cure of Sickness, - 82
XX. Affliction and Sickness, - - - - 86

CHAPTER.		PAGE
XXI.	The Great Physician,	89
XXII.	Our Duty in Case of Sickness	92
XXIII.	Responsibility,	101
XXIV.	Why not Accept Healing Now?	105
XXV.	Healing from a Desire,	110
XXVI.	Healing by the Word,	116
XXVII.	Healing by Inspiration,	121
XXVIII.	Trances.	126

CHAPTER I.

God is love. His infinite nature demands that all finite accountable beings should glorify Him; and His goodness strongly invites us to become partakers of His wonderful grace. He created an innumerable company of holy angels, and a great central world called heaven, in which they might eternally dwell with Him.

God's supreme majesty made Him the sole ruler of the angels and their home. Do you not wish we had such a home on earth? If so, then let us unite in praying, "Thy kingdom come. Thy will be done in earth as it is in heaven." Matt. 6:10. But alas, there came a time when one of the leaders of the angels dared to presume against the prerogative of God; and assumed that, inasmuch as his power had never been tested, he himself might be equal, if not superior to God. In the great and decisive battle that tested his strength God threw him out of heaven, at which

time he transformed himself into "that old
serpent, called the Devil." Rev. 12: 7-9.
Ever since that overthrow and transforma-
tion he has been the incessant enemy of
man, of angels and of God. As the poet
has said:

"Pride still was aiming at the blessed abode,
  Men would be angels, and angels would be gods;
  A striving to be gods angels fell,
  A striving to be angels man rebelled."

Thus it was by presumption, pride, and
rebellion, that the devil was originated, and
by his subsequent acts has caused the fall
of the human race, and all the misery
known to mankind.

God's love led to the creation of other
worlds than heaven, one of which (this
earth) became the abode of man. The
creation of man, like the creation of angels,
was designed for the glory of God. He
will protect all beings from evil whom He
creates, as long as they are true to Him. Inasmuch as all evil is from the hand of
Satan, and all good from the hand of God,
it became necessary that the Creator become the protector of His creature man
for good, and his safeguard against evil,
that he might fill the vacancy caused by the
angels that fell. 2 P. 2: 4. Good and evil

existed before the creation of man, as well as subsequently, and will continue to exist while the probation of man lasts. Therefore he must ever choose the right and reject the wrong. In fact, his eternal weal or eternal woe depends on his own choice.

"The tree of life" planted by God himself "in the midst of the garden of Eden," and afterwards seen in heaven by John (Gen. 2: 9; Rev. 22: 2), typifies Christ, who is to be obtained and retained only by entering into and meditating upon the things of God. "The tree of knowledge of good and evil" represents man's natural goodness in his fallen state, or the natural man out of Christ.

Presumption, or going outside of God's will to think or act, is eating of the forbidden fruit, which leads to the disfavor of our heavenly Father, to death, and finally to hell. O, beware of the tree of knowledge of good and evil, and eat only of the tree of life in the midst of the paradise of God. Beware of human philosophy and reason, the wrong use of which have robbed heaven, desolated the earth, and peopled hell. Surely "God hath made man upright, but they have sought out many

inventions." Eccl. 7:29. Yea, "Vanity
of vanities, saith the preacher, vanity of
vanities; all is vanity." Eccl. 1:2.

It is true, "The fool hath said in his heart,
'There is no God.'" Ps. 53:1. But the godly "delighteth in the law of the Lord; and
in His law doth he meditate day and night."
Ps. 1:2. If you would be godly, and not as
the fool, do not presume in reference to any
thing the Lord has not taught; but meditate
much on that which He has revealed by
His word, and by the Holy Spirit. If sons,
"Ye have an unction from the Holy One,
and ye know all things. The anointing
which ye have received of Him abideth
in you, and ye need not that any man
teach you: but as the same anointing teach-
eth you of all things, and is truth, and is no
lie, and even as it hath taught you, ye
shall abide in Him." 1 John, 2: 20, 27.

"If any of you lack wisdom, let him ask
of God that giveth to all *men* liberally, and
upbraideth not; and it shall be given him.

But let him ask in faith, nothing waver-
ing. For he that wavereth is like a wave
of the sea, driven with the wind and tossed.

For let not that man think that he shall
receive any thing of the Lord." James
1:5-7.

Therefore, as long as you maintain your cleansing by faith in the blood of Christ, and are led by the Lord, it is impossible for you to presume in reference to the things you do not know.

CHAPTER II.

MAN'S RELATION TO GOD.

We value things according to what they cost, and by the time we hope to keep them. God could have created millions of worlds of fine gold, or precious diamonds, without pain to anyone, and without sacrifice to Himself, but the redemption of a lost world cost Him "the brightness of His glory, and the express image of His person" —the Bright and Morning Star—the only begotten Son of God. Yea, God laid on Him the iniquity of us all, and forbade men and angels to save Him from the ignominious death of the cross. How great the sacrifice on the part of God, and how inexpressibly great the suffering of His Son when He cried, "*Eloi, Eloi, lama sabach-*

thani? which is, being interpreted, My God,
my God, why hast Thou forsaken Me?"
Mark 15: 34. How forceful the poet's words
concerning the sacrifice the Father made in
the giving of His Son to die for us:

> "Could I with ink the ocean fill,
> And were the skies a parchment made,
> And every stock was made a quill,
> And every man a scribe by trade,
> To tell the love of God above,
> Would drain the ocean dry,
> Nor could the scroll contain the whole,
> If stretched from sky to sky."

Yes, God is love; otherwise He would
not have given His only Son to suffer and
die in man's stead. But you ask, what is
man that God was so mindful of him?
Surely he must have been very precious in
the sight of God, or He would not have
ransomed him at such a wondrous cost.
Let us look prayerfully into this matter and
see if we can not know ourselves, and understand our true relation to the Creator. God
made man to do His will in earth as it is
done in heaven, and for nearly six thousand
years the Creator has been King and Ruler
of the world. His Son was born a king;
of a kingdom not of this world. Man
was created in the image and likeness
of God. It is said, "The proper study
of mankind is man." But this is not

enough, for man without God is like a train of cars detached from the engine. Hence, the proper study of mankind is man and his relation and responsibility to God. Man, like his Creator, is a trinity. He has a spirit, a soul, and a body; 1 Thes. 5: 23. These natures in Adam, prior to the fall, worked as harmoniously as the three persons of the God-head. The spirit, soul, and body, when adjusted to the will of God, are like a set of measures within and filling each other. The spirit dwells in, and fills the soul, while the soul dwells in and fills the body. The body is the house of the soul, and the soul the house of the spirit.

As a wise king rules his kingdom, so the spirit of man should rule his soul, and the soul the body. This world is man's kingdom. Gen. 1:26. As the world is his kingdom, it having been created and fitted up for him, so the body is the soul's kingdom, and the soul the spirit's kingdom. A kingdom without a king or ruler is like an army without a commander, not prepared to defend itself against foes, much less conquering its enemies.

The mental or intellectual man is the

soul which occupies the body and has
hands, feet, eyes, ears, and five senses within
the senses of the body. The heart of the
soul is the will, which dwells in the center
of its realm, which center is within the
physical heart, the king of the body. The
will is the king of the soul. Derange or
destroy the will and both soul and body
are dead as to the great end for which they
were created. The soul possesses all the at-
tributes necessary to perpetuate its existence
endlessly, independent of the body, which
dies when separated from it.

The moral man is the spirit that dwells in
the soul, and is either of Christ or of Satan,
because man is either a Christian or a sinner.
When God created man He placed His
likeness in his soul and His spirit in his
heart; thus God dwelt and reigned in the
heart of the soul as "King of kings and
Lord of lords." Rev. 19: 16. It is no mar-
vel that the sweet singer of Israel said of
himself, "I am fearfully and wonderfully
made." Ps. 139: 14. But alas! man has
fallen from under the hand of God into
the hands of Satan, who rules him soul and
body, as a tyrant king with an iron rod.
When man fell the image of Satan was

stamped on his soul, and the image of God was removed therefrom. Satan has taken such complete control of the human heart and will, that when one would do good, evil is present to prevent it. Rom. 7: 21. Yea, Satan has, with his poisonous fang, touched every human soul, and sown the seeds of disease and death in every human body. The poison of his sting brings moral death to the soul, physical death to the body, and damnation to both. "The wages of sin is death; but the gift of God is eternal life through Jesus Christ our Lord." Rom. 6: 23. In order to be saved the heart of man must be unreservedly surrendered to God. "My son, give Me thine heart." Prov. 23: 26. "Ye shall seek Me and find Me when ye shall search for Me with all your heart." Jer. 29: 13. Christ or Satan dwells in the heart of man, according as his will is. If a man wills to be saved there is no power that can prevent it; if he wills to be lost, there is no power that can save him. Salvation comes by saying, "Thy will be done"—damnation by saying, My will be done. Let God in the heart, and He will soon drive out all your and His enemies. Let Satan in your heart and he will

soon drive out all your friends and the
friends of God.

By conversion " the carnal mind " is removed from the heart, and the holiness of
God enters it to cleanse and reign therein.
Satan is cast out to make room for the birth
of Christ in the soul. The birth of Christ
within does not sanctify you wholly, but
you should seek to be as soon as born of
God.

CHAPTER III.

FALL AND REDEMPTION OF MAN.

Praise the Lord for man's salvation. Oh,
how complete and glorious it is. "As in
Adam all die, so in Christ shall all be made
alive." 1 Cor. 15: 22. The life received
by faith in Christ brings back to us all we
lost in the fall. Then let us "Give thanks
unto the Lord, for he is good; for His
mercy endureth forever."

The image of God, in which man was
created, was blotted from the soul of Adam
when he ate the forbidden apple. All his

posterity inherited from him a predisposi-
tion to sin—all his children's teeth are set
on edge.   Ezek. 18: 2.   All of Adam's
children that have arrived at the age of ac-
countability have followed the footsteps of
their father and have eaten of the forbidden
fruit; therefore every soul must have the
touch of the blood of the Lamb of God
who taketh away the sin of the world.   1
John 1: 7.   The salvation wrought out by
the Lord Jesus Christ covers all the natures
of man—spirit, soul and body.   It not only
casts Satan's image out of the heart, but re-
stores the image of God and makes it a fit
temple for the Holy Ghost to dwell in.   It
cleanses the triune man.   Matt. 6: 23; 8:16,
17; 10: 7.   Mark 3: 14, 15; 5: 8; 6: 13;
16:15–18.   Luke 4: 40; 6:19; 10:17; 13:11-
17.   "The very God of peace sanctify you
wholly; and I pray God your whole spirit
and soul and body be preserved blameless
unto the coming of our Lord Jesus Christ.
Faithful is He that calleth you who also will
do it."   1 Thes. 5: 23, 24.

God is omniscient.   There is no increase
of knowledge with Him.   All His laws are
in force until fulfilled.   Unlike man, He
never repeals a law on account of imperfec-

tion. When He first planned the scheme
of redemption it was as perfect as at present, and will be as perfect in the day of
judgment as in the beginning—no more so,
no less so. Eighteen hundred years experience in saving sinners has taught God
nothing; neither has the cleansing of the innumerable host of sinners lessened the
cleansing power of the blood of the everlasting covenant.

> "Dear, dying Lamb, thy precious blood
>   Shall never lose its power
> Till all the ransomed church of God
>   Are saved to sin no more."

The blessed Redeemer went about doing
good to all men everywhere; preaching the
Gospel to the poor and rich alike, healing
the sick and casting out evil spirits "with
His word." Matt. 8:16. It is the grand
privilege of God's ambassadors of the present day to accomplish the very same things
"in the name of Jesus Christ of Nazareth,"
and by the very same power they had at
Pentecost.

> 'Tis the very same power,
> The very same power;
> 'Tis the very same power
> That they had at Pentecost.
> 'Tis the pow'r, the power,
> 'Tis the pow'r, the power;
> 'Tis the power that Jesus promised should come down.

We have the same Christ to send us, the same great commission to preach, and the promise of the same power the Apostles had, and any failure to accomplish the same things will be wholly on the human side. The commission given to the Apostles was to hold good to the end of the Gospel dispensation—the end of time.

Hell was not prepared for man, but "for the Devil and his angels." Matt. 25:41. Nevertheless, all who die in the service of Satan must pass an eternity in his home, where the cankerworm of sin never dies, where the fiery torment is never quenched, and where the smoke of the torment of the damned ascends forever and forever. No one need hope for the salvation of Christ unless he complies with the Gospel of the grace of God, in which this salvation is freely given to all mankind. Friendly reader, how is it with thy soul? If Jesus should come to-day with ten thousand of His saints, with "the voice of the archangel, and with the trump of God," would it be well with thy soul? If not, then flee; flee to-day to the Rock that is cleft to take thee in.

How far short of his privileges and duties man has come. He is constantly leaving undone the things he should do, and as constantly doing the things he should not do. In the way of excuse for neglect and wrong-doing, some argue that some other way than the one marked out in the Gospel of God's dear Son will do quite as well. Such thoughts are suggested by the Devil.

> A constant watch the devils keep:
> They eye us night and day,
> And never slumber, never sleep,
> Lest they should lose their prey.

If the Gospel of the Son of God was preached and practiced by Christ's ambassadors of our day, as it was preached and lived by the blessed Master and His holy Apostles, Satan's empire would tremble from center to circumference, and the kingdoms of this world would soon be transformed into the kingdom of our Lord and Savior Jesus Christ. Instead of preaching the whole Gospel of Christ many have changed it to suit the religious dogmas of the day in order to please the itching ears of lukewarm professors. In so doing they check the work of God's grace, and hazard the souls of men. Oh, let us preach the whole Gospel and nothing but the Gospel, and live out the same—for then, and not until then, will this wicked world be brought to the feet of the blessed Re-deemer.

CHAPTER IV.

SALVATION BY CHRIST.

"Oh, horrible! A hell here! The flames around me! The fire within me! Burning, agonizing, dying! A hell to go to hell in! My God! But I have no God. I have re-jected Christ, and he who rejects Him re-jects the Father. Is there no hope for me?" "None but in Christ." "Then I am lost! O, hell, why did I choose you rather than heaven? O, Devil, why did I take heed to you, in preference to taking heed to God?"

"There is life for a look." "Where? How? When? Tell me, oh, ye who can, how I may escape the fire of hell, to which I am fast hastening?" "He that believeth on the Son hath everlasting life." "Ah, that's the trou-ble. Believe on Jesus—He whom I have spurned, defied and resisted all my life? No! no! After spending a lifetime, that was given me to love, worship and obey Christ,

2

in the service of Satan, the common enemy
of God and man, then to throw the snuffings
of a misspent life in the face of so good,
gracious and holy a being as God's Son, I
can not do it." "Then you are lost! *Forever
lost!*" "I know I am. Lost without hope,
plea, or remedy." "No! no! no! There is
hope, plea, and a remedy in Him whom
you reject. 'I am the way, the truth and
the life.' Look and live." 'O, the flames of
hell! My conscience, how thou dost goad
me! Why have I so long stood against
Him who still offers pardon and deliverance? Save me, good Lord, or I perish!"

"Hark! I hear a sound as of a chariot from
afar. Nearer it comes. Ah, I see its lone
occupant now. How pale he looks! His
sweat is like great drops of blood. His
hands and feet have imprints, as though
cruel spikes have been thrust through them.
His body is bruised and scarred, as though
He had been terribly beaten and maltreated.
O, God, I know who it is! It is Christ,
who died that I might have life. He suffered
this that I might escape the flames of hell,
and rise on wings of love to a mansion in
heaven. I will praise Thee for this coming
to me, if I am damned, O, thou Christ, the
Holy One."

"But I have come to save thee."

"Not me?"

"Yes, thee."

"But I am lost."

"I came to save the lost."

"Then, truly, Thou didst come to save me."

"I did."

"But, dear Savior, I have nothing to give —no merit of my own, nor none to recommend me to Thee for so great a salvation."

"Be quiet, my child; my gifts are free to those who accept them as such. Will you take salvation now?"

"I will. I do. I am Thine. Oh, glory! hallelujah!"

The sinner is in that broad and easy road that leads to the open mouth of a yawning hell. Jesus has made provisions to arrest him, by the Holy Ghost, in his mad career, turn him about towards heaven, and put a desire in his soul to run with patience the Christian race to glory.

Conversion includes justification, which is a change of state; and regeneration, which is a change of nature. The first is a work done for us; the second a change wrought in us. God is the author of both.

When God pardons a sinner He changes
his heart; so that the love of sin, as well as
the guilt of it, is taken away. Thus we see
when a sinner is converted he is justified
and renewed; his sins are blotted out and he
is made a new creature in Christ Jesus.
God, through love to man, not only pardons
and changes his heart, but He adopts him as
His child, puts him into His Church, and
sends the Holy Spirit to bear testimony
with his spirit that he is a child of a King,
an heir of a mansion, of a robe and a crown.

Repentance is essential to salvation. No
thief or murderer can enter heaven. There
is no other way to heaven but by Jesus.
You may try for another, but alas, it will be
a failure. Christ is the only source of salvation. If you go into one's house, you
want to enter by the door and not at the
window or through the roof. There is great
danger of being shot or kicked out as a thief
if you do. So in entering the Church of
Christ, if you would be recognized by God
and the angels, you must enter through
Christ—the door. The recording angel
keeps the register and no man can deceive
God. Earth's records do not save any. You
may deceive the world and yet live in hell,
but it is impossible to deceive God.

Every man must stand before God in the general judgment and render an account of the deeds done in the body. All must answer for themselves, and stand or fall according to their relation to Christ. If they have repented of all sin, and accepted Christ as their Savior, they stand justified before God and will be saved; if not, they will be lost—eternally lost. So all must repent or perish.

"Time enough yet," cries the oarsman, as his friend on shore warns him of the rapids below, into which he soon glides and is lost. "Time enough yet," shouts the inebriate, as he nears the awful gulf of a drunkard's hell. "Time enough yet," cries the sinner, as he dashes madly down into the flames of the damned.

"Too late," howls the demon, as his victim struggles to escape his fingers of death. "Too late," ejaculates the lost soul, as an angel reaches forth a helping hand. "Too late," wail all the unsaved sinners, as the flames of hell sweep over them forever and they are lost from earth, heaven, God, angels and the redeemed. Reader, is the above your photograph.

CHAPTER V.

THE NEW BIRTH.

Salvation from sin is the free gift of God, through the Lord and Savior Jesus Christ. It is to be obtained not by acts of righteousness which we have done or may do; (for "All our righteousness are as filthy rags." Isa. 64: 6.) but as a wholly unmerited gift of an independent king to an utterly unworthy and wholly dependent subject.

Grace first contrived the way
To save rebellious man,
And all the steps that grace displays,
Unfold the wondrous plan.

In order to salvation, one must believe himself to be a helpless and lost sinner, Jesus Christ to be the Son of God and only Savior, repent of his sins and turn to the Lord who will delight to have mercy, and to our God who will abundantly pardon. Isa. 55: 6, 7.

Before conversion the sinner has his back to Christ, to heaven, to angels and to God —his face to sin, to sinners, to devils, and

to hell—but when converted he turns his
back on the latter and his face to the former. Friendly reader, how is it with thee?
Is thy back turned to Christ, thy best
friend? Let thy heart answer in the secret
chamber of thy immortal soul. Remember that if thy heart condemns thee, God is
greater than thy heart and will condemn
thee, too. 1 John 3: 20, 21. When one
is born from above, God sends the Holy
Spirit into the heart as a witness to the
work done, and as an infallible guide to the
new-born soul. Rom. 8: 14-16; John
16: 13; 1 John 5: 10; 1 Cor. 3: 16; 6: 19.
"Ye must be born again," said the Master.

At the spiritual birth, "the carnal mind"
(which always is at " enmity against God")
is cast out, and the spiritual mind, which is
life and peace, is imparted to the soul.
Rom. 8: 6-8. This new spiritual life 'is
the body and blood of Christ, which the
dear Savior said we must eat of and drink,
in order to have spiritual life. John 6: 53.
This spiritual nature escapes with the soul
at death, and becomes the spiritual body;
which the soul inhabits until the final resurrection, at which time it will receive a glo-
rified body. I Cor. 15: 44. The new birth

is the beginning of the existence of this spiritual body within us, and is as real as was our natural birth, or the birth of the human nature of Christ. If true to God and our own souls, we will persevere until the carnal nature is cast out of both soul and body, so that the child Jesus born within may grow, until we are filled with all the fullness of God.

Turning from all sin with a full purpose of heart to forsake it, and turning to God with full purpose of heart to serve Him, constitutes evangelical repentance. The evidence of such repentance is confession of sin to God, and making restitution to those whom we have wronged, to the fullest extent of our ability. We are sorry to say that the latter evidence is too frequently wanting. See Luke 19: 8. This means far more than to join church, and live as thousands are living, with no spiritual life, no power.

We will close this chapter by quoting three golden invitations that fell from the lips of Him who spake as never did man: "Him that cometh to ME, I will in no wise cast out." John 6: 37. "In the last day, that great day of the feast, Jesus stood and cried, saying, 'If any man thirst, let him come to ME and drink.'" John 7: 37. "Come unto Me, all ye that labor and are heavy laden, and I will give you rest." Matt. 11:28.

CHAPTER VI.

TRINITY OF FAITH.

Faith, like the God-head, is a trinity in unity. In it we have asking-faith, receiving-faith, and overcoming-faith, following each other in the order just named. Asking-faith is given first. God gives this with each of His promises. He creates the desire in the heart of the sinner to come to Him. Except the Father draw the sinner he will not come to Jesus. John 6: 44. The desire to come, the knowledge as to how to come, and the asking-faith—all are of God. Asking-faith, and the knowledge how to ask, accompany each gift bestowed on man.

The way of eternal life has been made so plain and easy that they who neglect it are left without a single excuse. In the judg-

ment day all these will be as speechless as,
and share the fate of, the man who had not
on the wedding garment. Matt. 22: 12,
13. As the king furnished each invited
guest with a wedding garment, so the Lord
offers to furnish the garment of salvation
to each one who desires and asks for it.

Every desire created in the heart by God,
is a promise given by the Holy Spirit, and
points to man's need. When man is true to
God He will give him desires covering all
the needs of both soul and body. The
knowledge given with each desire shows
our need of the things desired. When God
gives a desire for a certain thing, He will
grant the thing desired. He never tantal-
izes His children with a blessing He does
not intend to give. Matt 7: 7–11.

To obtain the thing desired we must believe the desire is of the Lord, and ask for
the witness to this end. God's witness to
man is His will spoken in the soul by the
Holy Ghost. To get a desire cashed at
heaven's bank we must accept it as coming
from God, and ask for the witness to that
effect. In thus accepting a desire we make
up our minds to ask God to cash His check
at sight. Getting the consent of the mind

to ask, is the submission of the human will to that of the divine. It is marvelously strange that a great portion of the desires created by the Lord, or checks on the bank of heaven, are neglected or thrown away. How utterly foolish would he be thought who would reject or throw away a check for $100,000, signed by all the officials of the First National Bank of our city! How much more foolish is he who rejects or throws away a check on the bank of heaven for eternal life, when it is presented as a gift and signed by the Father, Son and Holy Ghost!

To ascertain whether a desire is from the Lord we must ask for the witness and hold on to God with all faith and knowledge received until we hear the voice of God speaking in the soul. Whatever the still, small voice whispers in the soul is the will of God and should be our guide.

The conscience in the Holy Ghost always speaks of our need of Christ. The Word says, " My God shall supply all your need according to His riches in glory by Christ Jesus." Phil. 4: 19.

To obtain the knowledge of God and the asking-faith from the desire, we must ask without doubting (" He that doubteth is damned." Rom. 14: 23.) for the witness, which is the word spoken by the Holy Ghost in the soul. When we ask God, from one of His given desires, with all the knowledge and faith accompanying it, if He will grant the desire of the heart, He always answers back in the desire—" Yes." When we hear the voice of God speaking in the soul, our faith leaps from the desire into the witness or word of God, and brings forth taking-faith, which enables us to receive the gifts offered by our heavenly Father.

Taking-faith is received with the witness from God from a given desire. Every witness given by God is accompanied by *taking-faith*, which is much stronger than *asking-faith*. In asking-faith we believe from a desire; while in taking-faith we believe in the word of God. There is great difference between belief *for* a thing and faith *in* that thing ; the latter is much the strongest. In the former we have the desire without the evidence, while in the latter we have both. Belief for a thing grows out of a felt want, and without internal evidence from God; while the latter has not only the external promise accompanying the desire, but the internal witness or Holy Ghost, bearing witness with our spirit that the thing desired is granted and awaits our taking. "What things soever ye desire, when ye pray, believe that ye receive them, and ye shall have them." Mark 11: 24.

Having received taking-faith, together with the knowledge as to how to use it, we should take the gift as coming from the God-given desire; therefore from God. In receiving God's gifts our faith becomes stronger than Satan's power of resistance. If our taking-faith is weaker than Satan's power it may be made more perfect and powerful. The trial of our faith, or per-fecting of it for greater power, is holding on to God and persevering through opposi-tion until victory is obtained.

To obtain power to receive God's bless-ings, and to do His will on earth as it is done in heaven, we must have perfect faith. When our faith is finished, by the trial of it, it will embrace "love, joy, peace, long-suf-ering," etc., and these rest upon us until the power is perfected within, when we should at once take the gift sought. We take the power, from time to time, as we are able to receive it, and the Holy Ghost gives the knowledge of it and tells how to use it.

Overcoming-faith will enable us to keep and use, to the glory of God, the gifts and graces He has so graciously given. This faith is as necessary to the Christian as asking-faith or taking-faith. Without it no one could retain or use the blessings received of the Lord. "He that overcometh shall inherit all things; and I will be his God, and he shall be my son." Rev. 21: 7. Overcoming-faith is received with the gift taken by asking-faith, which grows out of the desire given by the Lord. Asking-faith, when properly used, secures taking-faith, which, when used aright, secures overcoming-faith. We do not get over-coming-faith until we take the things desired of the Lord. God does not give one a thing he does not need. The promise is, "My God shall supply all your need." We do not need overcoming-faith until we have received something from the hand of God, Satan desires to take away from us. Rev. 12: 7–11.

CHAPTER VII.

FAITH AND WORKS.

All we need is freely provided by God. The body and soul need many things to save them from death and hell, and to prepare them for life and heaven. These wants are all met through faith and works. Both are essential. Faith and works should harmonize. As soul and body should agree in all things, so ought faith and works. Faith without works is dead. So is the body without the soul. God made provisions in the atonement for soul and body, so He has for faith and works. The soul and body are saved through these channels. Faith is the master, works the servant. In all things the master should rule. As the soul should rule the body, so ought faith to rule works. When this is done, and faith is made perfect through the truth, soul and body will be saved up to the standard of truth, as revealed in the Bible. We are saved "by grace through faith, and that not of ourselves; it is the gift of God." Eph. 2: 8.

According to our faith so is our salvation.

Man gets what he believes for. God has a
channel for everything. Man must seek
each needed want through God's channel to
possess it. All things are yours if rightly
sought for. Faith produces works. Believe
right and you will act right. The world is
full of unbelief. It is the damning sin of
the age. Devils believe more than some
professed Christians. "Lord, increase our
faith!"

Every spiritual blessing man enjoys comes
through faith. "By faith we live" (Gal.
1: 20.), "stand" (2 Cor. 1: 24.), "walk"
(2 Cor. 5: 7.), "conquer" (1 John 5: 4.),
"endure" (Heb. 11: 27.), "are sanctified"
(Acts 26: 18.), "are healed" (Mark
16: 17.), "and preserved to the end" (Heb.
10: 38.). There is no other way of prevail-
ing save through faith in God.

By faith, Peter walked on the angry
waves of the Galilean Sea to go to Jesus.
It was a wonderful walk. The life of faith
is a life of wonders. Our lives should be a
constant and close walk with God, hence a
life of wonder. Is it such with us? If not,
we are not walking with God as we should.
If our lives have nothing wonderful in them,
nothing to distinguish us from the world,

we certainly are not in line with the won-
der-working God.

The life of faith is above and beyond the
ordinary and natural life of man. Peter's
walking on the water was beyond his natural powers. Before this, no one (save
Christ) had ever walked on the water.
Thus it is, that those who walk close with
God are enabled to have an influence, and
perform deeds not possible to those who do
not walk with Him. "Enoch walked with
God," and "God took him" because he
walked with Him. Gen. 5: 24.

The walk of faith is a triumphal one. By
it we may have power to bring this world
to Christ. As Peter walked on the angry
waves of the sea, so we, by faith, may walk
on the angry waves of sin and not sink, but
bring Jesus across the angry waters of
death to perishing sinners that He may
take them in the "life-boat." If Christ calls
you, step out on His promises. Peter had
no power to support himself on the raging
sea; nevertheless he walked in perfect
safety as long as he kept his eyes on the
Master, but began to sink as soon as he
looked away from Him. So it is in the
Christian life; we must step out on the

3

naked promise of God, trusting in it to the
very letter, remembering that He has said
in His immutable Word, "My grace is sufficient for thee," "I will never leave thee,
nor forsake thee." 2 Cor. 12: 9; Heb.
13: 5.

There is a great difference between the
faith of many and the faith of the Son of
God. The faith we need is independent of
ours. Such faith sympathizes with the
poor, sick and distressed of our land. There
are two kinds of faith. Nearly everybody
has the general faith; but the faith not of
man is the faith we want. The reason why
so little faith is exercised is because we have
not the faith of the Son of God. When we
get this faith we will see great changes.

The presence of the Holy Ghost in the
soul gives the faith we need. It comes from
God—is of God. When we get it we will
have the same faith Jesus had. Faith is
taking God at His word. Then we can
laugh at seeming impossibilities and cry, "It
shall be done." The prophets made the ax
swim and the fire fall, by faith. "According
to your faith be it unto you," is a universal
law of God in bestowing gifts to His children. "All are yours," on condition you

receive them by faith. Are you believing for all God has done for you?

God's universal law is, that no blessing outside of those given in common to all men is available without the exercise of faith. Therefore, salvation from sin, or any of its effects on the spirit, soul or body, is received purely on the condition of a living, active faith in the atonement made once for all. In fact, Christ is "made unto us wisdom, and righteousness, and sanctification, and redemption," by our exercise of faith in Him, "who forgiveth all thine iniquities; who healeth all thy diseases." Ps. 103: 3.

CHAPTER VIII.

FOLLOWING JESUS.

God is able to save to the uttermost. He who can raise the dead, as he did Lazarus, can make alive those dead in sin, or heal those who are sick. Now give to God the things that belong to Him. Withhold nothing that is due Him. Many have vowed and have not paid their vows.

Glory to God, He is able to keep us. He

kept the three Hebrew children, amidst the
flames of the furnace, and He will keep us
if we trust in Him. Daniel was delivered
from the lion's den, Moses from the wrath
of Pharaoh, and David from the murderous
thrust of Saul. Fear not, but trust the living God.

The Devil trembles when he sees
The weakest saint get on his knees.

We were created for the glory of God.
Let us be true to Him, so that our words
and acts shall not surrender us to the Devil.
Give up the Devil's trappings. Step over
the line and trust.

Many cripple themselves through neglect
to testify to the salvation God has given
them. Honor God with your every-day
walk and life. If we do not, we dishonor
Him and hazard our own salvation. "These
are they which came out of great tribulation,
and have washed their robes and made them
white in the blood of the Lamb." Such,
only, shall enter the kingdom of heaven.

God sees us through and through. See
Him out on the barren mountain of sin seeking the lost. Behold, this is the day of
salvation. Ho! every one that thirsteth,
come and drink of the water of life. Haste
to Him now.

Heaven has millions of gifts for the saints of God. Have no hobby, but take them all. Be a whole Christian. Take the word of God. Everything of God is of revelation. We may have an experience that the gates of hell cannot prevail against. O, how many have they prevailed against! While we want the gifts of God, we need to be established in Christ's church—not my church, nor your church, but His church. "Upon this rock I will build My church, and the gates of hell shall not prevail against it." Matt. 16: 18.

Christ's church must receive the whole Gospel. They who deny any part of the Gospel turn themselves out of the church. If you do not understand God's church, keep your hands off of it, for you would better dig your own grave and bury yourself than attempt to steady the ark. He who rejects the ark, which is Christ in the saved, is liable to be stricken dead, as were Ananias and Sapphira. You may fight creeds, but you must never fight the Church of God; he who does it fights against God. It is death to do this.

The bride is the church of the first born. If we are converted to God we are espoused to Christ, and when sanctified we are married to Him. If we are married to Christ, and lust after the things of the earth, we commit adultery. The Holy Spirit wants to bring us back to chastity and purity. We may serve God in righteousness and holiness all the days of our life if we will let the Son make us free. "If any man keep My sayings he shall not taste death."

"Behold what manner of love the Father hath bestowed upon us, that we should be called the sons of God." So we sustain the same relation to God that Jesus does. For, beloved, now are we the sons of God, and if sons, then heirs—heirs of God and joint heirs with our Lord Jesus Christ. The glorious liberty of the sons of God is at hand.

Prepare to see His wonders, and see face to face and know as we are known. "He that hath this hope in Him purifieth himself even as He is pure." Christ came to take away our sin and sickness. Let us press through the crowd of unbelief as did the woman who touched the hem of Christ's garment and was made whole, and get healed of sin and all its contaminations. Let us do it now, for Jesus' sake. Amen!

CHAPTER IX.

ENTIRE CONSECRATION.

I beseech you therefore, brethren, by the mercies of God, that ye present your bodies a living sacrifice, holy, acceptable unto God, *which is* your reasonable service. Rom. 12: 1,

To be wholly and holily consecrated to God means a great work. Many do not comprehend, but think it a small matter. The above text indicates that the body, as well as the soul, is to be a "holy" sacrifice; that is to say, a pure one. To be consecrated to God, as were the Hebrew children, means something. They were ready to live or die for their Master. The consecration required is that of the Apostle Paul, when he said: "What mean ye to weep and to break mine heart? for I am ready not to be bound only, but also to die at Jerusalem for the name of the Lord Jesus." Acts 21: 13.

As Christ died once for all, so should we die to self and enter into an everlasting union with Him. When our all — spirit, soul and body—are laid on the altar of God,

Christ sanctifies the gift and makes us holy as He is holy.

Bible consecration means death to the world, death to the flesh, and an entire excommunication of the Devil from both soul and body. It means just what the dear Savior said when he prayed, "Thy kingdom come, Thy will be done in earth, as it is in heaven." Matt. 6: 10. Supreme love to Christ, and this only, will enable one to make such a consecration. The Hebrew children had this love to such a degree that they were willing to burn in the fiery furnace if it would please God. When our lives are "hid with Christ in God," then it is that He can and will trust us. Col. 3: 3. When thus consecrated we can pass through fiery trials victoriously.

In the natural and spiritual world life comes through death. The seed is cast into the earth and dies, and from its death springs new life. So, also, we must die to sin, that we may have a new life in Christ Jesus. Rom. 6: 11. In religion, to go down in the valley of humiliation is to get ready and to go up on the mount of spiritual transfiguration. "Whosoever shall exalt himself shall be abased; and he that shall humble

himself shall be exalted." Matt. 23: 12.
As a hill or mountain begins at every valley, so spiritual exaltation must begin at
every valley of humiliation. The deeper
the valley, the higher the exaltation. Here
we have natural law in spiritual life.

Bless the Lord for full and free salvation.
It is for all—none need be without it. The
floodgates of salvation to me have been
thrown open wide and my soul is basking
in ineffable glory. Hallelujah! But alas,
alas, multitudes are still walking in the
broad and downward road that leads to
eternal death and endless hell. O let us
plunge into the fountain filled with blood,
be cleansed from all sin, that God may use
us in rescuing the perishing. Jesus went
down into the garden of Gethsemane, pros-
trated Himself on the cold ground, agonizing
for us until His sweat was, as it were, great
drops of blood. He went to the death-line
and prayed, "Father, if it be possible let this
cup pass." It could not pass; therefore He
passed over the death-line, and voluntarily
gave Himself a living sacrifice for us all.

The Devil tried to persuade Jesus to not
sacrifice Himself, but He thrust him aside,
plunged into crucifixion and death, went

into the grave, rose triumphantly from it,
conquering the Devil, death, hell and the
grave, thereby securing eternal redemption
for us on the easy terms of His everlasting
Gospel. Are we willing to yield to death
to sin for Him who has done such great
things for us? The old man of sin must
die within us that we may be made alive
to God through Jesus Christ our Lord.

We do not get the salvation Jesus died
to obtain for us until we receive the Holy
Ghost. The sealing comes after pardon,
and is the inheritance of the believer. Could
you conceive of a more exalted position than
to sit in heavenly places in Christ Jesus?
This is the position He calls us to. Do not
put off your great privilege in Christ; for,
behold now is the day of salvation. Having
surrendered all to Jesus we are introduced
into the holy of holies, where all is peace
and joy in the Holy Ghost. Come, then,
to-day; for the night of death may overtake you this hour, and then it will be too
late. Too late—too late will be the cry;
Jesus of Nazareth has passed by. See what
wonderful power Peter had on the day of
Pentecost when he charged the Jews with
having slain the Lord of Glory. Where

from, and how did he get such wonderful power? He got it from heaven, and by tarrying, by praying and believing it would come.

> "'Twas while they all were praying,
> And believing it would come,
> Came the power, the power,
> That Jesus promised should come down."

So, also, we should tarry until we receive the Holy Ghost; then the same mighty works shall be done by us. If this should cause some to be put in jail it would doubt-less be the salvation of the prisoners and of many others. Lord, give us this sin-slaying and soul-saving power until all the socials, broom-drills, wheelbarrow-entertainments and all other works of the Devil are de-stroyed. God can take a worm and thrash a mountain. He can cause the Jordan to divide to let us enter the land that flows with milk and honey. When fully saved we can and will reach others. Men and women are sinking to destruction every day because we do not reach out and save them.

> Rescue the perishing, care for the dying;
> Jesus is merciful, Jesus will save.

CHAPTER X.

HOLY GHOST FIRE.

It is coming. Like the thunder's roar it may be heard. Yon vivid light, to one not acquainted with its destructive power, might be termed beautiful. But our opinion of it does not change its character in the least. On it comes. Death is in its track. Like perdition, it swallows up all it overtakes. See its darting tongue of fire. No mortal being can check or turn aside its onward course. My God, the great prairie is on fire! We are fifty miles from any known place of safety, and before one-tenth of that distance can be reached the flames will overtake us. Swift horse, run, run for your life, for the angel of death is on our track! But why go farther? You are already exhausted. I can hear your loud panting, and see the white foam bursting from your exhausted body.

Must we die? Is there no hope? Stop, horse, we can't outride the maddening

flames. Let us use the only known remedy. Let us fight fire with fire. O, for a
match, a coal, a torch, a little fire. But I have
none. Give me fire. Ever so little—so it
is fire. I must have fire. 'Tis fire or
death. My God, give me fire. I will give
you my watch, money, horse, farm, yea, all
I have, for fire. Vain offer. God's favor is
not to be bought by man's possessions.

Try it again. O, for fire! Great God, I
give myself to Thee; wilt Thou for Jesus'
sake, send me a little fire? Ah, that flash
of lightening dazzles me. But see, O, see
where it struck, the grass caught fire!
Glory to God, we have got fire. I thank
Thee, O God, for heaven-sent fire. It has
saved me. Roll on, thou nearing flames, I
fear thee not. Thou mayest rage like the
flames of hell, rolling out to destroy sinners, but I am safe. As safe as the soul
from which the Holy Ghost fire has burned
out all sin; for to such the flames of hell
can not reach, nor in such can they find any
thing to burn.

This way, good horse, keep close to me.
Let our breath fan on the heaven-sent fire.
It is burning faster and faster. Let us fol-
low it up close. There, by lying on our

faces, we will now be safe. But we will trust God for more. The breath of the sea of fire fans on our saving fire. See how it spreads and gathers power at every breath. It is already a great fire. Up, good horse, we may now, in safety, stand on yon burned spot, and shout defiance to a million prairie fires.

Wonderful! Surrounded by a sea of fire. The two have met, yet we are safe. Hallelujah! The fire that threatened our lives is already dying out, and the one in answer to prayer is out-ranking it in brilliancy and power. Thus God's fire outranks Satan's, as His power does the power of the great arch fiend. So now, dear horse, we may pass on our way over this burned district in as great safety as a blood-washed soul can traverse this sin-cursed earth on his way to the paradise of God.

God's fire can burn out and destroy all sin. Cast all on the altar and it will sanctify the gift. "Be ye clean, saith the Lord." O Lord, let Holy Ghost fire fall on all the people. It is a thousand times better to have the Holy Ghost fire burn all sin out of us than to have the fire of sin burn in us

in hell forever and forever. If we get all
sin out of our hearts, hell will not have us
at any price. Both sin and holiness will
seek its level and its own.

God is omnific and equal to any emer-
gency. When fully trusting in Him one
can walk through a den of lions. Satan
did not have in the beginning, has not now,
and never will have power equal to or superior to God. The Devil is to be "cast into
the lake of fire and brimstone, where the
beast and the false prophet are, and shall
be tormented forever and ever." Rev. 20:10.
Daniel slept soundly among the blood-
thirsty lions, with angels for his body-guard.
The Hebrew children walked through the
flames of the furnace, and came out without the smell of fire on their garments.
Likewise may Christians now walk through
the flames of sin without being contami-
nated with it. Are we fully saved? If
not, why? We cannot serve God with
perfect acceptability until we are wholly
given up to Him, spirit, soul and body.
Oh, for the holy fire—sin-killing, carnal-
consuming fire! More of this fire, and less
preaching of theories, is the great need of
to-day. Lord let the fire come on all the

people and destroy all sin. FIRE! FIRE!!
FIRE!!!

CHAPTER XI.

PURITY OF HEART.

The destruction of the carnal nature or
effects of sin is as much the work of God
as is the pardoning of the sinner. This work
follows the former (if only a second), and is
done instantaneously. Upright living will
not destroy the effects of sin, neither will
sickness, sorrow or death. Jesus alone can
do this. He who has the power to purify
a soul, can keep it pure. Purity of heart
is a holy state, and is to be obtained by a
full and complete consecration to God. He,
seeing our faith and act of consecration,
applies the cleansing blood, and the work
is done.

We never can grow into a state of purity
of heart, because growth implies adding to
that which already exists; while this purity
is obtained by taking from, or the removal
of carnality or the effects of sin from the
soul. In the work of redemption, the first

act is that of giving eternal life to those who are dead in trespasses and sins; the next, the exchanging of carnality for holiness in the soul; and the next the purification of the body for the reception of spiritual power to glorify God. These three experiences follow each other in the order named, though it may be but a second apart, and must all be received before God's will is done in earth as it is in heaven. Matt. 6: 10. After these are received the work of maturing the spirit, soul and body in all the Christian gifts and graces may, and should be carried on in Christ Jesus forever.

It was in a vision, or trance, that Ezekiel saw a holy stream of water running out of the Lord's house. As it ran, it became broader and broader, deeper and deeper, until it was a mighty river, that he could not pass over. Ezek. 47: 1–5. The life of every Christian should be like this stream, ever growing broader and deeper, as it flows on toward the City of God. The reason many Christian lives flow on so feebly is because there is but little Holy Ghost power in them. The unconverted soul is spiritually dead, and can no more send forth spiritual life than a dry fountain can send forth pure water. It is not enough that a fountain have water in it; it must be filled full to the very top before it can flow out in a stream to gladden the earth. So it is with the Christian; he must not only have the Holy Ghost in his soul, but should have it filled full up to the very top, then when God pours in more grace the fountain of living water will flow out and bless others. Friendly reader, how is it with you? It is useless for the sinner to seek purity of heart first. Nothing short of pardon, regeneration, adoption, and the witness of the Holy Spirit will prepare one for the reception of purity of the heart.

All the works of God are perfect. He gave us a perfect Savior, a perfect Gospel, and requires a perfect life at the hand of each of His children. As gold is purified by the fire, so God's children are to be cleansed from the last and least remains of sin by the Fire of the Holy Ghost. The ore must first be found, then dug out, then crushed, then burned in the fire, until the refiner can see his image reflected in the metal—then it is pure. So it is with the sinner; he must first be found (for by nature he is lost), then dug out of the pit of sin,

then crushed by conviction, then burned in
the crucible of the Holy Ghost until the
image of the divine Refiner (the Savior)
appears in his heart, then the dross, the sin,
is all consumed. Mal. 3: 3.

Being born of God, the converted soul, if
true to Him, soon develops to man or woman-
hood, and, through love, is sanctified or married to Christ. The marriage relation includes a
voluntary contract, which can not be made
before birth or after death, so sanctification
is a voluntary state, entered into between
Christ and a free moral agent, and must
take place between one's spiritual birth and
natural death. Before conversion the soul
is dead in trespasses and sins. At death its
probation ends. So in either case the soul
is not eligible to enter the marriage relation
with Christ. As one marries to dwell with
his companion, and not to die and be separated, so should every converted soul at
once enter the holy of holies, and dwell
with God here on earth, while He wills it,
as well as forever in heaven.

CHAPTER XII.

THE EXTENT OF SALVATION.

Once I was lost, but now am found; was blind, but now I see. When lost, I was a child of Satan, but when God found me I became His child. I was saved through the sufferings, death and blood of Jesus Christ.

What did wash away my sin?
　Nothing but the blood of Jesus.
What did make me pure within?
　Nothing but the blood of Jesus.

CHORUS.

Oh, precious is the flow
　That makes me white as snow;
No other fount I know—
　Nothing but the blood of Jesus.

In my hands no price could bring—
　Nothing but the blood of Jesus.
Simply to His cross did cling,
　Nothing but the blood of Jesus.

I cheerfully accepted the offer of salvation as a free gift from the crucified hands of Jesus—then He took me up in His blessed arms and plunged me deep down in the fountain filled with His own precious blood, and when I came out was whiter than snow. Thus saved, I am to have eternal life, instead of eternal death; eternal heaven, instead of eternal hell.

Many, through ignorance of their privileges in the Gospel, come to Jesus for pardon and cleansing of their souls, but leave their bodies still in Satan's dominion. They bring the sin-sick soul to Him to be regenerated and sanctified, while they leave the diseased body, which was made so by sin, still in its deplorable condition, and thereby thwart the will of God. A healthy body is often as necessary to God's service as a sanctified soul. For instance, a man is dying without Christ, you alone can win him to Christ. He sends for you, but alas, the Devil is lashing your body with a burning fever, so that you cannot go to the sick man, and he dies and sinks to hell because you neglected to exercise faith in God to keep your body from disease, or, when afflicted, to go to the Great Physician and be cured. Souls are perishing day by day, all around us, because God has not got active children to reach them.

This doctrine Jesus taught the Apostles they were to teach to others, and their successors to others, and so on down to the end of the Gospel dispensation—the end of

time. This old Gospel cannot be improved
on by men, by angels, or God. In the
scheme of redemption God gave us His
best wisdom, best love, and best gift of
heaven. How fearful the blunder when
our great city paper said, "The methods in
vogue with these emotional brethren, and
often alluded to as 'old-fashioned religion,'
will in time give way to *more quiet, modern
and improved plans of saving souls*."

When the Savior sent the Apostles out on
the limited commission "He gave them
power against unclean spirits to cast them
out, and to heal all manner of sickness and
all manner of disease." He also said to
them, "Heal the sick." Matt. 10: 1, 8.
When He sent forth the seventy He in-
structed them to "heal the sick." Luke,
10: 9. When the Master gave the Apostles
His farewell commission He told them to
"cast out devils," to heal the sick, and He
would be with them to the end. Mark 16:
17-19. We are under the old Gospel dispensation—let us walk strictly according to
the old paths—the old-time religion, and
expect the blessing of the very same power
they had at Pentecost.

CHAPTER XIII.

PURIFICATION.

Purity fits man for the reception of spiritual power. The strength or power of almost everything depends largely on its purity. As steam is the combined strength of fire and water, so is purity the combined strength of the gifts and fruits of the Spirit. 1 Cor. 12: 8-10; Gal. 5: 22. As will and muscle are necessary to action, so justification and sanctification are necessary to purity. Purity is the beginning of spiritual power. One can only receive and use power in proportion to the extent of his or her purity. In preparing the Apostles for their great life work the divine Master breathed on them and said, "Receive ye the Holy Ghost." John 20: 22. After this, on the day of Pentecost, they were filled with the Holy Ghost. Acts 2: 4. All power for good belongs to God. Purification embraces the whole man, spirit, soul and body. The desire for purity is created by

the Lord, and if followed out may be
blessed to the receiving of purity of soul
and body. Thus the whole man is perme-
ated and filled with purity—the power of
God. Purification of the body is obtained
by degrees, because our gifts and graces are
all received that way. These degrees
should be taken as fast as God gives the
desire and knowledge concerning them.
"Whosoever is born of God doth not commit sin, for his seed remaineth in him"
(Jesus being born in him by the Holy
Ghost), and can not sin because he is born
of God." 1 John 3: 9. Therefore when born
of God we should ask for heart purity, and
hold on by the rope of faith until we receive it. Receiving heart purity, like conversion, is an instantaneous work, but the
coming to it may have been the work of
years. The receiving of purity of body, as
we shall proceed to explain, is gradual.

When God created man, He gave him a
body as an essential part of his being; and
his usefulness and happiness depend on
the physical man. Therefore let us present our bodies a living sacrifice, holy, acceptable unto God, which is our reasonable
service. Rom, 12: 1; Matt. 5: 29; 1 Cor.

6: 15; 9: 27; 1 Thes. 5: 23; Dan. 3: 28;
Rom. 8: 23; Phil. 3: 21. To get this over-
flow, or power, from the soul into the
body our wills must be completely subju-
gated to the will of God. That is to say,
we must agree to let God forever have
complete control of our bodies for His
glory — His temple. Our wills must be
swallowed up in His will for time and eternity. There must be no mental reservation
whatever. Having thus submitted our wills
to God, we must steadfastly hold on to His
promise until we receive the purification
sought.

The *trial* of faith purifies the soul, and
the tried or finished faith causes the power
to pass into the body and purify it. When
this is done God gives the witness of entire
purification, which is the third grace. Acts
4: 23-33. It is the finished work of faith
that takes the power into the body. This
perfection comes by degrees as we become
able to bear it. The trial of faith and the perfection comes in like manner. 1 P. 1: 7.
When God perfects the first degree of
purity, or that which we are able to bear, He
gives us the witness of the Holy Ghost to
this effect; and so on from one degree to

another until all the gifts and graces He has for us are received, then it is we receive the witness of the Holy Ghost, that the work of God within us is complete in every respect, and we receive a divine shock from the divine battery, that fills us from finger tips to end of toes. Yea, then it is we are filled with all the fullness of God, and with Paul can say, "I am crucified with Christ, nevertheless I live, yet not I, but Christ liveth in me; and the life which I now live in the flesh I live by the faith of the Son of God, who loved me and gave Himself for me." Gal. 2: 20; Col. 3: 3; 1 Cor. 3: 22; Rom. 8: 38. In perfecting the work of purity from spirit to soul, and from soul to body, God carries out the natural law seen in all His works of utilizing and working by means already produced. Thus it is we should advance from strength to strength in faith, from strength to strength in power, and from strength to strength in love. The strength of faith works in the strength of power, and the strength of power in the strength of love. O, the wonderful salvation of the blessed Jesus Christ! "Eye hath not seen, nor ear heard, neither have entered into the heart of man, the things which God hath prepared for them that love Him. But God hath revealed them to us by His Spirit, for the Spirit searcheth all things, yea the deep things of God." 1 Cor. 2: 9, 10.

CHAPTER XIV.

THE ANOINTING POWER.

"Ye shall receive power, after that the Holy Ghost is come upon you; and ye shall be witnesses unto me both in Jerusalem and in all Judea, and in Samaria, and unto the uttermost parts of the earth." Acts 1: 8.

The anointing power is of God and is given only as man's natures are made pure by the blood of His Son, and it will be used to His honor and glory. When justified by God the spirit of man is a receptacle for divine power, which should be secured at once. When sanctified the soul is ready to receive the anointing power, and when purified the body is ripe for it. The anointing power enables us to enjoy and use the gifts and graces received from God to his honor and glory.

Every man, woman and child should be cleansed from all sin and filled with God's love and power. When thus saved and filled ye are holy. "Ye shall be holy; for I the Lord your God am holy. Therefore, follow peace with all men and holiness, without which no man shall see the Lord." Lev. 19: 2; Heb. 12: 14.

The triune man, when wholly the Lord's, is cleansed from all sin and filled with divine love and power. The spirit is holy when man is born into the kingdom of God; the soul, when freed from the effects of sin and sealed up with Christ in God; and the body when purified by the blood of the Lamb. Thus the triune natures of man are made partakers of the divine nature and have access to unlimited power in Christ Jesus, who has all power for good in heaven and earth. Hallelujah!

To receive the anointing power in your soul and body the very God of peace must sanctify you wholly.

The word sanctification, including its de-

rivatives, occurs in the Bible more than one
hundred times. Few words expressive of
Christian experience occur as often. This
doctrine is taught to a greater or less extent
by all the leading denominations of this
country; and for so doing we have a thus
saith the Lord: "This is the will of God,
even your sanctification." 1 Thes. 4: 3.

It is a holy state, including spirit, soul
and body. 1 Thes. 5: 23. This was Adam's
normal state prior to his fall. Can not this
blessed state be secured now by all his posterity? We know of no reason why every
part of man's trinity should not be holy and
live to glorify God. All those who are fully
sanctified walk, talk and live in harmony
with the blessed Savior in all things. They
do not become offended at the truth, neither
are they moved about by every wind of doctrine, but are rooted and grounded in the
faith of the Son of God. Perfect sanctification is separation from all evil, and the
setting apart of spirit, soul and body to the
service of the Master. It is a rending of,
and passing through the veil, or religious
dogmas of men—an entering in through the
door (Christ) into the will of God—a set-
tling down and sealing of the entire man to
God.

Sanctification emanates from Jesus Christ, (1 Cor. 1: 30.) and is carried on by the Holy Ghost. Rom. 5: 16. God give us a sanctification that will make us one according to the Savior's intercessory prayer. This will reach all the affairs of government and each individual of the same. Christ desires perfect oneness among His people that the world may believe that the Father hath sent Him. John 17: 20, 21. The great truths of the Holy Scriptures should be repeated over and over, until they are riveted on the minds and hearts of the children of men—all men.

The spirit of a good man craves those things its nature demands; but the spirit of a wicked man craves the things that will eternally ruin it; "For, to be carnally minded is death; but to be spiritually minded is life and peace. Because, the carnal mind is enmity against God; for it is not subject to the law of God, neither indeed can be." Rom. 8: 6, 7.

No one can be in a justified state and still possess the carnal *mind;* but he may be in that state and still have the carnal *nature,* or effects of sin on soul and body. The carnal mind, which is the heart of the spirit, or king of the body of sin and death within us, is Satan himself, and must be removed to make room for the conception and birth of the Son of God within us.

There is a vast difference between the *carnal* mind and the *carnal* nature, or effects of sin on soul and body. The former in-cludes the exercise of the will, while the latter does not. Satan, as king of the spirit of the unsaved, dwelling in the will, or king of the soul, often induces the will to gratify the spirit's nature and thus causes the indi-vidual to sin against God. Justification frees the will from this enemy, the image of Satan in the spirit; pardons the guilt, and arrays the soul's king (the will) against the carnal nature, which inclines to evil, but cannot produce an act, for which one is re-sponsible, only by the consent of the will. Paul did not say to the "babes in Christ," at Corinth, "Ye are carnally minded" (for to be carnally minded is death), but he did say: "I speak not unto you as unto spiritual, but as unto carnal, even as unto babes in Christ." 1 Cor. 3: 1.

CHAPTER XV.

HOLINESS.

God has a holy people. They are the Redeemed of the Lord; have been washed in the blood of the Lamb, and shall not be forsaken, nor their land desolated; but they shall be called Hephzi-bah, and their land Beulah. For the Lord delighteth in them, and their land shall be married. For as a young man marrieth a virgin, so shall thy sons marry thee, and as the bridegroom rejoiceth over the bride, so shall thy God rejoice over thee. Even the Gentiles—the children of this world—shall see their righteousness, and all kings their glory; and they shall call them by a new name, which the mouth of the Lord shall name—"The holy people"— while they eat and praise the Lord in the courts of His holiness. These holy ones shall be a "crown of glory" in the hand of the Lord and a royal diadem in the hand of their God. Therefore, go through the gates; prepare ye the way of the people; cast up the highway; gather out the stones; lift up a standard for the people; say ye to the daughter of Zion, "Behold thy salvation cometh!"

Son of man, go speak to the children of thy people, and say unto them, "Behold the Lord has called you to be holy as He is holy; therefore, He hath set watchmen upon thy walls, O Jerusalem, which shall never hold their peace day nor night, till thou come into the courts of His holiness and art a praise in the whole earth."

Thank God for "The Holy City," which John saw "coming down from God out of heaven," "that great city, the holy Jerusalem, descending from God out of heaven;" and for the "great voice out of heaven saying, 'Behold the tabernacle of God is with men, and He will dwell with them, and they shall be His people, and God Himself shall be with them and be their God. And God shall wipe away all tears from their eyes, and there shall be no more death, neither sorrow nor crying. neither shall there be any more pain; for the former things have passed away. And the nations of them which are saved shall walk in the light of it, and the kings of the earth do bring their glory and honor into it.'"

Glory to God for a holiness which admits us within heaven's jasper walls, golden streets and gates of pearl. Yes, holiness is the password, and it alone shall admit us, for though "the gates of it shall not be shut at all," "there shall in no wise enter into it anything that defileth; neither whatsoever worketh abomination, or maketh a lie; but they which are written in the Lamb's Book of Life."

O, will not holiness be popular then? Think of it! a great city filled with an innumerable multitude which no man can number, all worshiping God in the beauty of holiness. Not an opposer or unholy one there. Where, O, where, then, will these opposers of holiness ("without which no man shall see the Lord") be in that day when Christ comes to make up his jewels? Alas, will they not, with the rich man, lift up their eyes, being in torment—in the flames of hell—and cry for these holy ones whom they once despised, called hard names, and persecuted, to bring them a little water to cool their parched tongues?

CHAPTER XVI.

PRESERVATION.

"The very God of peace sanctify you wholly; and I pray God your whole spirit, and soul, and body be preserved blameless unto the coming of our Lord Jesus Christ. Faithful is He that calleth you who also will do it." 1 Thes. 5: 23, 24. In order to be preserved blameless until the coming of our Lord Jesus Christ, the very God of peace must sanctify us wholly. When born of God, the spirit's king is Christ, who is holy, having sanctified Himself that we might be sanctified through the truth. John 17: 19; 1 John 3: 9. The soul enters the kingdom of God within us through Jesus Christ the door, and is made holy, for nothing unholy can enter there. Likewise may the body be made holy by purification and be kept blameless until the end of our probationary state.

God hedges the perfect man about from the wrath and power of Satan, so that he' cannot destroy him. Job was thus protected—the Devil could not touch him only as God permitted. Job. 1: 8-12; Ps. 23:

1-4. Jesus said to his despondent Apostles, "Let not your heart be troubled; ye believe in God, believe also in Me. In My Father's house are many mansions; if it were not so I would have told you. I go to prepare a place for you; and if I go and prepare a place for you, I will come again and receive you unto Myself, that where I am, there ye may be also." John 14: 1-3. This statement is a direct promise on the part of the blessed Savior to protect in life, and in the end to bring the Apostles to the paradisical, blood-washed throng.

Jesus is so faithful, and the atonement He made so perfect, that not a single one of all He has forgiven need fail to reach the beautiful land beyond the Jordan of death. Praise the Lord! "Know ye not that ye are the temple of God, and that the Spirit of God dwelleth in you? If any man defile the temple of God, him shall God destroy; for the temple of God is holy, which temple ye are." 1 Cor. 3: 16, 17. "Him that overcometh will I make a pillar in the temple of My God, and he shall go no more out; and I will write upon him the name of My God, and the name of the city of My God, which is New Jerusalem, which cometh down out of heaven from My God; and I will write upon him My new name." Rev. 3: 12. God's saved ones are temples on the earth, and are to be pillars in His temple above.

The wall of salvation (Isa. 26: 1; 60: 18.) in which the fully saved are to be preserved blameless unto the coming of our Lord Jesus Christ, is composed of three inde-structible walls. The inner wall is "the blood of Jesus Christ" which "cleanseth from all sin." 1 John 1: 7. Satan can not pass the blood of Christ. Yea, he fears the blood of the divine Redeemer, for it is a swift witness crying from five bleeding wounds against him. The middle wall is the "word of God." Heb. 4: 12. When Satan tempted Jesus in the wilderness, He smote him each time with "the sword of the Spirit, which is the word of God." Eph. 6: 17.

The outer wall is composed of fire. "Our God is a consuming fire." The Devil dreads the fire, knowing he is to be cast alive into a lake of fire burning with brimstone. Rev. 19: 20.

God surrounds all whom He wholly sanctifies with the wall of fire, the wall of truth, and the wall of blood; either one of which is so strong that Satan can not pass through without the consent of the will of the soul.

CHAPTER XVII.

SOUL AND BODY WORK.

The Gospel of the blessed Savior teaches the only true religion; and is destined to prevail over all other systems. As the Gospel of Christ teaches the only true religion, so He is the only Savior. All who reach heaven will get there through and by the Lord Jesus Christ. In His atonement the same provision is made for the body as for the soul. As faith in Christ removes the sin of the soul, so will faith in Him remove sickness of the body. The everlasting Gospel teaches that all should look to Christ, and to Him alone, for salvation from sin and its effects on both soul and body. The provision made for the healing of the body is as free and complete as that provided for the healing of the soul.

An eminent writer says that the provision made for soul and body is the same; and that just to the extent that the soul may be cleansed and kept from sin, so may the body be healed and kept from sickness. The extent of the cure of the soul and body, and the keeping of them pure, depends on the faithfulness of the people in laying hold of and appropriating the means of grace provided.

If, therefore, with the ample provision made, any are sick who are not delivered and preserved from sickness, the fault is wholly their own; and it is simply because they do not avail themselves of the most abundantly provided and freely offered grace of the Gospel.

The healing of bodily diseases, through the prayer of faith, is a supernatural, rather than a miraculous gift. The Scriptures make a marked distinction between the gift of healing and that of working of miracles.

"But the manifestation of the Spirit is given to every man to profit withal.

"For to one is given by the Spirit the word of wisdom; to another the word of knowledge by the same Spirit;

"To another faith by the same Spirit; to another the gifts of healing, by the same Spirit;

"To another the working of miracles; to

another prophecy; to another discerning of spirits; to another *divers* kinds of tongues; to another the interpretation of tongues;

"But all these worketh that one and the selfsame Spirit, dividing to every man severally as he will." 1 Cor. 12: 7–11; 28–30.

In no case of Christ and His disciples healing ordinary sickness is it mentioned in the Gospel as a miracle. Nearly all the mighty works that Christ and His followers wrought for the human body and mind were classed under the head of supernatural, rather than miraculous healing. The raising of the dead, curing the lame, dumb or blind from birth, and similar works, are often classed as miracles. But the healing of bodily diseases and sickness, strictly, is never classed among miracles.

In all cases of miracles and supernatural healing, God's power alone insures the result. There is a diversity of gifts conferred on man, but all by the same Spirit. Whether the cure is reached by a word, or a touch, by anointing with oil, or the laying on of hands, or the prayer of faith, it matters not; it is God's power that works the cure or produces the result.

The Scriptures teach that the healing of

the sick is supernatural, and place it along-
side of the healing of the soul, from sin. In
the physical and spiritual realm, the healing
of disease and sin is the direct power of the
Holy Spirit. So that the healing of the
sick is as binding on the believer to-day as
is the preaching of regeneration and sanctification.

If the term miracle, as applied to the
healing of the sick, was discarded, and its
treatment placed among the works of the
Spirit for the body, the same as conversion
and sanctification is for the Spirit and soul,
it would be placed just where God intended
it to be. "Himself took our infirmities and
bore our diseases." So we see that the healing of the body of disease, and the soul of
sin rest upon the solid foundation of the
atonement, and from this standpoint, and
this alone, should be taught and received until
the end of life. Christ did not provide a
partial, but a complete deliverance for all His
people. The atonement was made for the
relief of the body as well as for the soul, so
that Christ's children may be delivered from
"all manner of sickness and all manner of
disease" just as completely as they can be
"cleansed from all sin." The basis and pro-

visions are the same for the body as for the soul. Therefore, it is not a partial but a complete deliverance that is provided and freely offered to all His believing children.

CHAPTER XVIII.

SICKNESS AN ENEMY.

God has always treated sickness as an enemy. Some people differ with God; they look on sickness as a means of grace, ordained by Him to promote the sanctification of His people. And yet they will run to a doctor and swallow ever so much medicine to be cured. Oh, how foolish it is to claim that all disease is of God, to promote one's salvation, and then swallow medicine to thwart God's plan. Away with such nonsense. The Scripture always speaks of bodily disease as an evil, coming from the Devil as a result of sin. It is never called a blessing, an ordinance of God, or means of grace. The Old and New Testaments alike teach that all sorts of disease are of the Devil.

It is true that disease and sickness are sometimes set forth in the Scriptures as a judicial infliction, and as a chastisement or rebuke, and as a reminder of our departure from God. So is sin used to alarm and bring people to Christ. Yet no one will say that wickedness is ordained as a means of grace. This would make Satan our Savior instead of Christ. It is the Devil's theology repeated that we must sin a little daily to keep ourselves humble and in constant need of a Savior.

All sickness is of Satan, and never of God. It is true that God always tries to overrule it, as He does all sin, for our good. God chastises His children for their wrong doings as a true parent does his disobedient children. Yet no one will claim that the parent made the child do the deed for which he was chastised, or that any good parent will chastise his obedient children.

The fact of the case is, that God is love and never wilfully punishes any one. He has created man, and for his protection, become his governor, which includes both law and a penalty for its violation. The Devil,

God's enemy, hates whatever God loves, and through revenge is ever seeking to get man to violate God's laws. Therefore the Devil, and not God, is the author of all sickness, sorrow, pain and death, as these are but the natural results of a broken law.

The Devil knows that God's laws are just, and that the penalty for their violation must be inflicted or all law would be at an end and God's government would totter and fall. So he, by every strategy known to his vocabulary of tricks, is ever seeking to lead man to violate God's law. Satan has two objects in thus leading man. The smaller is, man's affliction and, if possible, his destruction. The greater is, to get God, if possible, through His intense love toward man, to cease executing justice and thereby overthrow His government. This trick the cunning fox tried on God through Adam, and again through Christ in the wilderness.

God has made certain just and good laws to rule and protect His children on earth. The Devil often gets them to violate these laws. The righteous Judge sees that these laws are executed. Man suffers the penalty. The Devil triumphs. God is defeated. Who is to blame, the Judge, the criminal, or the instigator of the crime committed? In a moment one man slays another. It was a wilful murder. Twelve honest men, before whom the murderer is tried, so declare it. The judge, in behalf of a violated law, pronounces the penalty. The sheriff, to carry out the law, hangs the murderer by the neck until he is dead. The law, "He that sheddeth man's blood, by man shall his blood be shed," has been executed. Two citizens of our commonwealth have been ushered into eternity, and to whom are we to look for redress? Not to the murderer, for he is gone; not to the judge, jurors or hangman, for they did their duty in the matter. Who, then, is responsible for these two lives?

"'Our Father, which art in heaven,' is it you?" "No, no, my child! I, through love to them, gave my Son's life to save them."

"Dear Savior, is it you?" "No; I taught them to love one another, and finally died for them that they might inherit eternal life, and you know no murderer hath eternal life."

"Was it you, loved Holy Spirit?" "Oh, no; I am the Comforter, sent into the world by the Father and Son, on the one mission of saving and not destroying men."

"Devil, was it you?" "Ha-ha! Me! Why,
I feel like eating you up!"

"Murderer, speak from thy home of un-
quenchable fire, and tell us what led thee to
this rash act of thine?" "Ah, 'twas Satan,
the prince of liars! I listened to him, and
am here! He is responsible for the loss of
the two lives. I was only his obedient tool
in the awful tragedy. He is the author of
all sickness, sorrow, pain and death! Destroy
him, and you forever stop it all."

All sickness, sorrow, pain, death and hell
are from the same source. The author of
one is the author of all. They are all fruits
of sin. If you make God the author of any
one, you must make Him the author of all.
If the author of all, then there is no personal
Devil, nor hell, and evil is only good mis-
placed.

The Devil wants to be worshiped. He
offered Christ the whole world if He would
worship him. One of his strategies to get
worshipers is to get people to ascribe his
works to God, and in worshiping the author of these acts of his he is worshiped.
Thus, Job unwittingly worshiped the Devil
by blessing the author of his sickness, and
thus every one is worshiping him who

ascribes sickness, sorrow, pain or death to God, when they are all of the Devil.

If the Devil gets us to recognize sickness or any of its results as of God, he drives a wedge between us and Christ; for if we ascribe to God the sending of these as so many remedial agencies, then Christ is not the only source of salvation, but the author of these becomes a part of it, and as Satan is the author, he becomes our savior in proportion as we recognize his saving virtues in his afflictions. And, be assured, Satan will claim his own at the judgment day, if not before. For the moment you admit anything outside of Christ as a remedial agent, you detract so much from Him who bore our sins and sicknesses on the tree. The Devil wants us to recognize some merit outside of Christ, so that He is not received as our complete salvation. Anything that claims merit for our salvation outside of Christ is of the Devil. All disease is of the Devil; it is the result of sin. If Satan can get you to say, as he did Job, that the Lord has done what he himself is doing, he has you as he got possession of Job, and oh, how he did torment the poor man! The Devil wants us to think that all disease comes from God, so that we may worship him as its author instead of applying to God for its removal. Do not let the Devil, dear reader, deceive you any longer, but when sick ascribe it to him and go at once to God and get a cure.

CHAPTER XIX.

CAUSE AND CURE OF SICKNESS.

"The prayer of faith shall save the sick." James 5: 15. Are there any sick? Let us see. This world has 1,300,000,000 souls. Of these, one dies each second, and, on an average, the whole of the world's inhabitants every thirty-three years. Go from house to house the wide world over, and we meet sickness on every hand. Why is this? Did God create man to suffer and die? Haste to His Word and see: "So God created man in His own image; in the image of God created He him; male and female created He them." Gen. 1: 27. Was God ever sick? No. Did He ever die? No, no. Then neither was man created to sicken or die, and had he never sinned he never would have experienced sickness, sorrow, pain nor death.

The cause of sickness is sin. No sin, no sickness. This was Adam's experience before sin entered the world, and will be the experience of all when sin is banished from it as it is from heaven. Sickness is not always the fault of the afflicted. It may be inhaled, absorbed, swallowed in food cr drink, or inherited.

Sin is a violation of God's law; sickness is one of its results. God does not make laws for man that he, by His aid, can not keep; nor does He cause him to break them for the sake of punishing him. Hence, all law-breaking and its results are from an enemy. God is not the author of sin; therefore sin and its results are of the Devil. Sickness is the result of sin; therefore sickness is of the Devil, and never of God. The cure for sickness is the same as the cure for sin. "They brought unto Jesus many that were possessed with devils, and He cast out the spirits with His word, and healed all that were sick, that it might be fulfilled which was spoken by Esaias the prophet, saying, 'Himself took our infirmities and bore our sicknesses.'" Matt. 8: 16, 17. Inasmuch as Christ took our infirmities and bore our sicknesses, we do not need to bear them, because He is our burden-bearer. Jesus can heal the diseases of the body just as easily as He can forgive the sins of the soul. Mark 2: 9. The atonement of the Savior was for bodily infirmities as well as for the sins of the soul. Therefore I preach healing for both soul and body—this is the way Jesus did. He never forgave the sins of a sick, or blind, or lame man without curing his body also. He always treated disease as an enemy. He commanded His Apostles "to preach the kingdom of God and to heal the sick." Luke 9: 2. In the last great commission Jesus said to His Apostles: "And these signs shall follow them that believe. In My name shall they cast out devils." He also said, "They shall lay hands on the sick, and they shall recover." Mark 16: 17, 18. There is no statement in the Bible that this commission has been revoked or in any degree changed. Until a change is made by divine authority, we are duty bound to teach just what Christ taught concerning this matter.

Jesus has, by the shedding of His precious blood, purchased many gifts for His people, and one of them is that of healing bodily infirmities. It stands on the promises as does that of pardon, or cleansing. They are all based on the death of Jesus.

Pardon, cleansing and healing are blessings promised by a multitude of passages of Scripture. These are among the positive gifts for all who have faith to believe and ask for them. The only hinderance to conversion, sanctification or bodily healing is unbelief.

Sin is opposed to righteousness; therefore no one need expect God to heal the sinner. This would be to add strength to the enemy. To be healed, we must first seek the kingdom of God and His righteousness. None but true Christians can offer the prayer of faith; therefore, if you desire to be healed, you must come in the way of the divine appointment by the prayer of faith, anointing with oil or the laying on of hands.

The question has been asked, "Can God replace missing limbs?" To this we would answer, Yes, if He desires to do so. However, such an act would be one of creation rather than redemption. The atonement was made to redeem that which had already been created, and forfeited through the fall. Therefore the replacing of missing limbs is not a matter of faith-healing, but of creation. Faith-healing is not miraculous, but supernatural. It is restoring wasted or afflicted parts of the body.

We understand a miracle to be something outside of and beyond the usual course of nature, or grace; while faith-healing, or the healing of the sick in answer to the prayer of faith, is, or should be, a common occurrence; for it is in direct harmony with God's law of grace.

CHAPTER XX.

AFFLICTION AND SICKNESS.

I am sick. O, these aching pains! How long, O Lord, must I suffer? Is it for Thy glory that I am called to suffer, or is my pain the result of having violated some of Thy laws? Is it Thy will that I should thus

suffer? I have searched Thy Word and no-
where can I find where Thou hast laid affliction on Thy obedient children. On the
other hand, I find that affliction and sickness are often sent on those who are disobedient to Thy will. Are parents responsible for the wickedness of a wayward
son? Certainly not, if they did all they
could to bring him up in the fear and
admonition of the Lord. Has not God done
all He could to save men? Yes. Then
He is not in any way responsible for the
diseases and suffering of mankind; for they
are the result of violating God's laws. Disease, like carnality, may be hereditary, and
yet cause the individual to suffer as severely
as though he or she had wilfully violated a
known law.

O, how important that we should walk
with God, as did Enoch, and learn how to
care for our bodies and souls, so that when
our stay here on earth has ended our spirits
may be safely gathered home to God, with
the blest assurance that in the resurrection
day our bodies shall be fashioned like unto
the glorious body of our Lord and Savior
Jesus Christ.

There is a marked difference between

affliction and sickness. James says: "Is any among you afflicted? Let him pray. Is any sick? Let him call for the elders of the church," etc. Afflictions are of various kinds. An eighty-year-old saint recently testified: "I am well, but afflicted. God has healed my body of all disease, but I feel the infirmities of old age fast creeping on. Oh, for the resurrected body!" Yes, the resurrected body will always be young and free from infirmities.

In 2 Tim. 1: 8, Paul speaks of the afflictions of the Gospel. He suffered much through preaching the word of God. All the Apostles (but one) lost their lives by opposers of the Gospel. If we were as bold as they were, some of us might be added to the long list of Christian martyrs. Paul was writing, as God's prisoner, to Timothy, not to be ashamed of the Gospel, the preaching of which had, through wicked men, brought him to prison, but to be the more zealous for God, if it cost him bonds, or even death.

God knows no compromise with sin, nor should any of His subjects. He who lives godly in Christ Jesus shall suffer persecution. Therefore, my brethren, count it all

joy when ye fall into divers afflictions for
Christ's sake, knowing that if they have
done these things to the green tree (Christ),
it is liable to happen any time to the dry,
(yourselves).

CHAPTER XXI.

THE GREAT PHYSICIAN.

When Jairus' daughter took sick he went
out in the city of Capernaum to beseech the
Savior to come and heal her. While on his
way he was overtaken by one of his ser-.
vants, who informed him that his daughter
was dead, and suggested that he should not
trouble the Master, because it was too late
for Him to render her any assistance. This
messenger had about as little faith in the
ability of Jesus to heal as many Christian
people of the present day. As soon as Jesus
heard that Jairus' daughter was dead He
turned to him and tenderly said: "Be not
afraid, only believe." Mark 5: 35. How
simple the terms of healing for both soul

and body; "only believe, only believe,"
that is all—how simple.

When the Centurion met Jesus he said:
"My servant lieth at home sick of the palsy,
grievously tormented; *but speak the word
only and my servant shall be healed.*" Matt.
8: 6, 8. These words are so full of faith
that they are worthy to be printed in gold.
The Master said He had "not found so great
faith; no, not in Israel."

As a tender father flees to the assistance
of his children when afflicted in body or
mind, so also does Jesus flee to the assistance of all who are afflicted, and never fails
to give the needed relief when He is called
on in faith.

> The great Physician now is near,
>   The sympathizing Jesus,
> He speaks the drooping heart to cheer,
>   Oh, hear the voice of Jesus.
>   CHORUS.
> Sweetest note in seraph song,
>   Sweetest name on mortal tongue,
> Sweetest carol ever sung,
>   Jesus, blessed Jesus.

The reason why some who are healed
soon relapse apparently into the same sickness, is the same which causes so many,
whose conversion is undoubted, to soon become cool in love, weak in faith, or lapse
into open sin.

Our bodily diseases, as well as our spiritual maladies, are atoned for by Christ. The healed body is as liable to relapse as is the converted soul. According to your faith, so it shall be. If faith in the bodily cure become weak, either after or during the progress of recovery, a relapse into sickness would be most natural. "The just shall live by faith."

When looking to God for bodily healing, all other agencies should be abandoned. The same common sense should be exercised as when under a physician. No good physician will take a case unless the patient agrees to follow his directions and take his remedies.

A failure to take a physician's prescription will not only prevent a cure, but will dishonor him, and prevent others from going to him to be healed. So it is with Christ; if we do not take the prescription He gives, and as directed, we dishonor Him, prevent a cure and discourage others from coming to be healed. If you take medicine while trusting the Lord for a cure, and recover, to whom are you going to give the credit, God, the druggist, or the physician? You see at once the inconsistency of the whole matter. "Ye can not serve two masters."

No true Christian should charge God with
afflicting him. When God does afflict it is
useless to run to an earthly physician to be
cured.

If we do not believe that Jesus will heal
our bodies, as well as our souls, do we not
dishonor Him and His word, and in so doing
commit a sin. When the Apostles failed to
cast the Devil out of the lunatic child, Jesus
rebuked them because of their lack of faith
in Him. Matt. 17: 19-21.

CHAPTER XXII.

OUR DUTY IN CASE OF SICKNESS.

"Good morning, Doctor Calomel."

"Ah, quite well, I thank you."

"My cold is getting worse, Doctor."

"Very sickly times, I assure you."

"O, dear, I hadn't heard of it!"

"The people are dying everywhere."

"Ain't you successful in your practice?"

"Very; I made $20,000 last year."

"Indeed! But have you lost any patients?"

"Only those who have died, and, of course, they could be of no use to me any longer."

"Then you doctor to make money?"

"True; and so does all our craft."

"Doctor, what do you do with a rich patient?"

"Keep him sick as long as practicable."

"If the patient is poor, what?"

"Then I let him get well, or kill him off, as deemed expedient."

"Why do you keep the rich sick?"

"The longer the sickness the larger the fee."

"You never continue the sickness too long?"

"Yes; but the estate pays my bill, all the same."

"But do not you lose by his death?"

"It is all considered in his bill."

"Why do you kill off the poor?"

"To save time to devote to the rich."

"Why not get them off your hands by curing them?"

"None but God can cure diseases."

"Then why do you practice medicine?"

"For the same purpose that you farm or sell goods."

"Ah, I see; you make people sick that you may live."

"Yes; others sick, if not sick, that I may live."

"Well, Doctor Calomel, what is my bill?"

"O, wait till you are well, and we'll see."

"But you say none but God can cure sickness."

"True.   Yet He has created remedial agencies."

"Yes; but He who put healing virtue in the plant can bestow it direct."

"Very well; but the unbeliever will trust us when he won't God."

Are you a Christian?   If so, the inspired Word tells exactly what you ought to do in case of sickness, when those having the gifts of healing cannot be secured.   1 Cor. 12: 9.   "Let him call for the elders of the church." Jas. 5: 14. The Word does not give the sick believer the choice of calling in a physician, patronizing a druggist or calling for elders to anoint him, but in commanding words, "Let him call for the elders of the church."   Therefore, if any of God's children are sick, it is their duty, when no one possessing the gifts of healing is available, to call for the "elders."

The elders here required are God-made, and differ greatly from those who are only made such by man. They are men or women endued with the prayer of faith for the restoration of the sick. They are such persons as are matured in the doctrine of healing and practice it effectually.

"Let them pray over him, anointing him with oil," is the elders duty. The oil used in primitive times was olive oil, and may be found in almost any drug store. There is no healing virtue in the oil or in the hands laid on, only as God operates through them. In case only one elder can be had, God honors his prayer of faith as much as when more are present. Experience teaches that it is better to be alone while offering the prayer of faith than to have unbelievers present. Matt. 9: 25; 2 Kings 4: 33.

A believer should be anointed each time he gets sick, unless his faith immediately grasps successfully the promise of healing without it. No believer need be anointed twice for the same disease unless his faith fails before the cure is effected, and he afterward concludes to try again. If there are any symptoms of the disease after the anointing, the prayer of faith or laying on of hands might be repeated daily until they disappear. God never wants a physician to be called

and our systems drugged with poisons. He
proposes to be our physician, and does not
want any rival in the work. If you can not
trust the Lord, then you may go to the physician and take your chances, which is better
than nothing.

The Bible speaks of physicians only four
times: First, of Joseph getting one to em-
balm his dead father (Gen. 50: 2.); second,
King Asa trusting them instead of God, and
dying (2 Chron. 16: 12.); third, Job declar-
ing, "Ye are all physicians of no value" (Job
13: 4.), and fourth, of suffering many
things of physicians (Mark 5: 26, and Luke
8: 43.). Concerning physician see Jeremiah
8: 22, Matthew 9: 12, Mark 2: 17, Luke
4: 23; 5: 31, Col. 4: 14. Now, in all these
you see no command or recommendation to
earthly physicians, but rather a leading
away from them to the decisive healer,
Jesus. Luke may have practiced medicine
before his conversion, but there is no account, or even hint, of his doing it afterward. Of medicine the Bible speaks only
once (Prov. 17: 22.), which merely shows
there is virtue in it when properly used,
which is for sinners who will not turn to and
trust God.

DIED OF STARVATION.

"Poor Jones," said a quaint writer, "died of starvation, although worth $50,000. I'll tell you how it was. Jones was always fancying that there was something the matter with him; so he went to a physician one day and had himself examined, and the physician told him he had the kidney disease, and that, besides taking medicine, he must diet himself. Said the physician: 'You must avoid all kinds of salt meats, salt fish, potatoes, cabbage and vegetables of every kind.' Jones followed the advice, but found himself no better. He went to another physician, and after being examined, was informed that he must avoid all kinds of fresh meats also. This did not do him any good, as he thought, and he went to another physician, who highly approved of the advice which had previously been given, and further warned him against all kinds of pastry, likewise shell-fish, including oysters and clams. 'The best thing for you is a milk diet,' said this physician; so Jones lived wholly upon milk. Not feeling himself any better, he went to another physician, who cautioned him to avoid milk above all things, if he wanted to get well. This reduced Jones to a diet of cold water and fresh air, and, finding himself no better under this regime, he went to another physician, who advised him to beware of drinking too much water and being too much in the air. This last advice cut off the last of Jones' articles of diet, and he died of starvation, as I told you."

Why did not Mr. Jones do like the woman who "suffered many things of many physicians," turn to the Great Physician, who never fails to cure, and that too, without money and without price.

The believer's commission concerning healing of the sick embraces the following duties, viz.: Praying in faith for the afflicted (James 5: 14.), anointing them with oil (James 5: 14.), and the laying on of hands (Mark 16: 18.). The promise is that they shall be healed and their sins forgiven them. When Jesus healed Peter's mother-in-law, He laid His hand on her (Matt. 8: 15.); when He healed the sick people at Nazareth, He laid His hands on them (Mark 6: 5.); when he healed the deaf and stuttering man, He put His fingers in his ears, spit and touched his tongue (Mark 8: 32, 33.); and when He opened the eyes of the man who was born blind He touched his eyes by anointing them (John 9: 6.). God's glory demands that His children should conform to His methods of curing their bodily infirmities as well as their spiritual diseases. If disease is brought about by violating the laws of nature, said violation must cease before God will heal the afflicted. This is true concerning both soul and body. In either case there is no promise of help from God until the transgressor turns from the evil of his way. When recovering from sickness by the power of God, the individual should be as careful to observe the natural laws as if the convalescence was brought about by medicinal aid.

Have all earthly physicians failed you? Do not be discouraged, but look up to the Great Physician whose skill has never been baffled. His knowledge, skill and power to heal are exhaustless.

It has been reported that President Garfield was fed on morphine and whisky, and all ministers excluded, while the Christian world was called on to pray for his recovery. If this be true, how could we expect God to heal the dear man? In this the

7

children of Satan point to his death as a
test case concerning the power of prayer
and say, "It is a failure." God is not responsible for the death of James A. Garfield, because his case was not submitted to
Him as the Scripture requires. A physician
can not be made responsible for the recovery
of an individual until the case is fully re-
signed into his hands and his directions followed.

In seeking for bodily healing the afflicted
should discard all medicinal agencies and
submit the ailment wholly into the hands
of God.

On returning home from a day's toil the
author was met by his wife at the door, and
exclaimed: "Oh, I am so glad you have
come. Mary is very sick; she came near
dying a little while ago with an awful spasm,
the same as Johnny had when he died.
What shall we do?" "Dear wife," I exclaimed, "we must not distrust Jesus, let
happen what will. We trusted two of our
children to the physicians, and they both
died. Now we will trust little Mary to Jesus,
and she shall live." Accordingly, we both
knelt before the Lord and offered the prayer
of faith for her speedy recovery. Our faith

was tested. Satan endeavored to bring on another spasm. Again we wrestled with God. This time faith triumphed. Jesus turned back the power of Satan, rebuked the disease, and it vanished. God triumphed. The Great Physician wrought the cure, and to God be all the praise, now and forever. Amen.

[The author has received "the gifts of healing," (1 Cor. 12: 9; Matt. 10: 5-8; Luke 10: 1, 9, 17, 19.), and has laid hands on hundreds of people who, by so doing, were healed of "all manner of sickness and all manner of disease" by "the power of the Lord." Matt. 6: 23; Luke 5: 17. A great many people have been healed by sending him their handkerchiefs. Acts 19: 11, 12. Should you desire his help in salvation meetings on this line write to him at 334 North California street, Indianapolis, Ind.]

CHAPTER XXIII.

RESPONSIBILITY.

Man is responsible for his own sins and sickness to the full extent of his ability to have avoided them. He is responsible if he fails to apply for the remedy provided in the atonement of Jesus Christ. He is also responsible for transmitted sins, and transmitted sickness to the full extent of his ability to have avoided them.

While man is responsible for his inherited and transmitted sin and sickness, only so far as he might have known and applied the preventive and cure, nevertheless each violation of God's spiritual and physical laws demands a penalty whether done wilfully or through ignorance. Hence the suffering of soul and body on account of a broken law, known or not known, and the need of an all-powerful restorer.

Owing to ignorance, one may be holy and die of sickness as the result of sin. The sin of sickness may result from one's own disobedience to natural laws; or it may be like inbred sin, inherited. A great deal of sin is inherited. Thus the sins of the parents are visited on the children to the third and fourth generation. O, what a fearful responsibility rests upon parents, both as to their own health and that of their children!

God holds us responsible for all the evil we could have prevented. In the atonement ample provision has been made for our release from all sin, and for preservation from sickness.

All sickness is the result of sin. Remove
it from the world and sickness will disappear. In heaven there is no sin, therefore
no sickness. But, says one, the best of saints
are often afflicted by disease as much as are
sinners. You are mistaken; the best Christians are sick but little, for they trust God
for both health and salvation. Says another:
"Are not Christian people often terribly
afflicted?" Yes, and often much more so
than children of the Devil, for while they
have learned to exercise saving faith for
their souls their bodies are left for Satan to
destroy, which he delights to do.

If Satan can not destroy your soul, he will
take vengeance on your body if you will let
him. If he loses the soul he will afflict
the body all he possibly can, both to gloat
his hatred toward God, and to keep you
helpless in Christ's service. Satan boasts
of the strength, riches, power and activity
of his followers, while he points the finger
of derision at the poor, weak, sickly child
of God. I tell you a child of God should
not be sick. If sick he should go to God
and be healed. If sick when saved, Satan
will retain him in sickness if possible, and
if well, will afflict him through revenge

and in order to weaken his force in the service of his Master.

By sin and sickness, Satan has succeeded in shortening man's average life from seventy to thirty-three years, instead of letting him live out his allotted time of three score years and ten, and then depart this life in peace as a result of old age.

But you say many get sick who do not sin. Well you can not prove it, for all sins are not open to man. But in order to investigate further we will admit that many get sick who do not sin, which fact proves nothing for you, as all are affected by sin in the soul from birth, and vast multitudes inherit disease as well. The diseases of the parents are inherited by the children for many generations. Your sickness does not prove that you have sinned, neither does it prove that it is not the result of sin. Your sickness as well as your depravity may be inherited. No one claims that depravity is not the result of sin, because they did not produce it, nor have they any right to claim that all sickness is not the result of sin, because the afflicted did not commit the sin that caused the sickness.

CHAPTER XXIV.

WHY NOT ACCEPT HEALING NOW?

"A loving child, you say?"

"Yes; the most so of all my children."

"And you love him in return?"

"I do, as only a father can love."

"How long has the young man been sick?" ·

"Three years and a half."

"Ah! Isn't it awful?"

"True, my brother, for his suffering is terrible."

"Why don't you cure him?"

"Oh, sir, I have tried every available remedy, but he steadily grows worse."

"Then you would heal him if you could?"

"Certainly; for I love him as my life, and 'all that a man hath he will give for his life.' "

"Does your boy love Jesus?"

"It is his greatest joy to talk of Him."

"And Jesus loves the boy?"

"Sir, I know He does. Didn't He die for my child?"

"And no doubt would like you to do all in your power to help him?"

"To be sure, for His love is greater than mine; I never died for any one."

"Won't Jesus, then, heal your son if you put him in the Great Physician's hands?"

"Why, surely He would; for all power is given unto Him on earth and in heaven, and I would if I only had the power."

"Then take him and all your sick at once to Jesus, and have them healed. Surely you are a very cruel father to have your son suffer so long, and a never-failing remedy ever at hand."

"Ah! I stand rebuked, and justly, too; for while I have spent a fortune with earthly physicians, which means might have been used in the salvation of many souls, I have not trusted Jesus, the Great Physician, for a moment with the cure of my son. But I will do so no more. Here, wife, pour out the drugs, and let us get down before God, and receive Jesus as the healer of our boy. Thank God, He heals now—even now! Amen!"

Jesus loves to heal and to save to-day.

Why, then, do you wait? Will you be better prepared to accept His blessings by waiting? Then how foolish and useless to expect to be prepared by waiting or deferring to some other time that which you ought to accept now.

The Devil's time for us to claim deliverance never comes. "Wait until to-morrow; you are not quite ready to be saved or healed," is his most frequent argument. Thus time flies, while Satan's time never comes, and the poor sufferer is kept looking to Satan's time instead of to the world's Savior, for his deliverance from the effects of sin. Remember, suffering ones, that "now is the accepted time; now is the day of salvation." This is God's time, while the Devil's time never comes.

Why so many failures? All around us are those who have apparently embraced Christ's word, and for a time run well, and then fall entirely away. Such cases bring reproach on God's cause. They embrace soul and body. After seeking healing of God and obtaining relief from suffering, they cease believing for a perfect cure, and remain feeble and incapable of active service all their lives. Try to arouse them, and

they say it would be presumptuous to ask
for more, or that they are patiently await-
ing God's time to finish the work.

The Devil is a liar. Beware of his angelic
guise! His masterpiece is to keep us out of
the fullness of our inheritance by a false
humility, a presumptuous patience. Oh,
how many, through ignorance of Satan's
devices, are abiding his time instead of the
Lord's. Cruel monster! How I loathe him.
Thus day by day and year after year thousands of suffering ones are cruelly delayed
from obtaining the will of God.

Christ's work is a finished one. We are
to be living epistles of His finished work.
This we can never do by a half-and-half
fulfillment of His will concerning us. We
find no half finished work wrought by Jesus during His ministrations on earth. "As
many as touched Him were made perfectly
whole." Then do not wait to become
better, but at once lay all on the altar of
consecration. Reckon yourselves dead to
sin—all sin. Do it now!

We have a right to claim God's promises
as long as He permits us to live. The
promises secured by the atonement are not
lost to us, simply because we may have out-

lived our three score and ten years. If we live beyond this, we have as good a right to lay our sicknesses on Jesus, who bare them for us, as we had before that time. Therefore as long as we live in the Lord, we may, and ought to ask Him, if sick, for healing.

Healing does not depend on being present, where united prayer is offered for healing. The healing comes by grace through faith, and not as a result of being present with those offering the prayers of faith. Knowledge of the way of faith healing may be had at faith meetings; and the presence of those who have faith often stimulates our own, so that by this help many are healed, who failed until they learned the way of trusting at faith meetings. If God so loved us, that He gave His Son to die for us, "will He not with Him also freely give us all things." Yes, most assuredly. Then think not thyself of so little importance to the Lord that He would not even work a miracle, if needs be, to keep thee on earth a few days longer.

CHAPTER XXV.

HEALING FROM A DESIRE.

In receiving healing from God, the power used must be greater than that used by Satan in putting the disease on you. We need have no fear on this point, because Jesus said: "All power is given unto Me in heaven and in earth." To overcome the Devil, we must be the strongest, which we can not be only as God gives us strength. "Ye shall receive power after the Holy Ghost is come upon you." Acts 1: 8. As man yields to the will of God he becomes partaker of the divine nature; and as he partakes of this nature he comes in possession of superhuman power.

Jesus came into this world to destroy the works of the Devil. Why, then, is it not done? Because the salvation of man, as to both soul and body, depends on his faith; and the faith in God is wanting. God's power to save or heal men works only in proportion to their faith. Matt. 13: 58.

Therefore we do not wonder that the Apostles prayed, "Lord, increase our faith."

Jesus heals diseases now on the very same terms as when He was here among men, viz.: by the diseased coming to and having faith in Him; for, "without faith, it is impossible to please God," much less to obtain His power to heal.

The different ways of healing set forth in this and the next two chapters are for the purpose of teaching how to obtain a faith stronger than Satan's power in our disease. When God creates within us a desire to be healed we should take Him at once as our healer. With each desire He gives asking-faith and knowledge as to how to ask. All desires that are from God are so many promissory notes made payable on sight at the throne of grace.

If we seek healing from the desire only (which contains all things promised on condition that we seek until found), we should accept the desire as coming from God, and believe at once for the things desired, and not let go until He opens it up in answer to our petition. Whenever a desire for healing is opened by God in answer to the prayer of faith, whether from the desire, or in the witness, or by inspiration, the more powerful methods of divine healing, we should at once take healing with all the faith at command and give God the glory.

In obtaining healing from an open desire, the power of God comes out of it and enters the disease. The cannon ball leaps from its mouth and speeds on its way to execution in proportion to the strength of the powder that sends it forth. So it is in healing; the power of God is exerted in our behalf in proportion to the strength of our faith. As Aaron's rod (by the power of God) became a serpent and swallowed up the magicians' serpents, so the power of God, carried by a faith that is stronger than Satan's power, will swallow up disease.

The desire (in which is God's power containing our healing) being opened by the dear Savior in answer to our prayer of faith, gives the opportunity to take the healing at once. It was locked up in the desire so you could not get it. Now you can—will you take it? Say, "By the grace of God, I will." If you thus decide, you and Satan will have a conflict, and you might as well prepare yourself for the battle. "Put on the whole armor of God that you may be able to stand against the wiles of the Devil." Eph. 6: 11.

It requires grit, grace and great perse-
verance to thwart and overcome the Devil.
Therefore, we should be as determined to
take healing as Satan is that we shall not be
healed.   Having fully determined to receive
healing of the Lord, we should see that our
faith has sufficient power to overcome and
destroy Satan's works.   Have strong faith
in God and be bold against Satan, and you
will be sure to triumph over him.   Two
armies are arrayed against each other. One
is your disease, carried by the power of
Satan according to his will; the other, your
healing, carried by the power of God according to your faith.   As the powder carries the bullet, so your faith carries the
power of God.   God deals with man as a
free moral agent, and leaves him free to
take healing or reject it.

If, in the battle for healing, your faith is
weaker than the will of Satan in the disease, it lets God's power fall below Satan's,
and the disease continues to rage.   If the
power of God and the power of Satan are
equal, your healing and the disease stand
still facing each other like two gladiators.
But if your faith is greater than the will of
Satan in the disease, the power of God goes

above the disease and swallows it up, while your healing in God's power leaps out into the body, giving you health.

If faith from the desire fails to secure healing, then your faith should be tried for the taking of greater power. The trial of faith is the completion of it for the taking of power, while the development of a finished faith is the using of it for God's glory. Should you fail to receive healing from a tried faith, you should go forth and take it by impulse, for "the kingdom of heaven suffereth violence and the violent take it by force." Matt. 11: 12. You should be determined to conquer or die, for if God does not destroy the disease it will kill you. "All that a man hath will he give for his life." Shout "To arms! To arms!" and close in on the enemy. "Be ye angry (at Satan) and sin not," instinctively becomes your motto for the moment, as you leap at the Devil's throat in the disease, and with all the power your concentrated faith commands, try to choke the very life out of him. Have no pity on "Old Satan," but wage a war of extermination on him, and if your faith is stronger than his power in the disease, you will be healed and put him to flight. Never yield; if defeated once, try again, and continue to try until your faith is sufficiently developed to swallow up Satan's power. While there is life you should never yield to death's demands, for it is an enemy—the last one to be overcome. Enoch and Elijah (by the power of God) triumphed over death, without passing through it. God will do as much for us; but in reaching the zenith of our glory we may be called to walk through the valley and shadow of death—only the shadow, thank God! Your desire proves that God wants to heal you. If you have sought to be healed and failed, it is because your faith was too weak to take the necessary power from God to destroy the disease. Therefore try again. There are lengths, breadths heights and depths in faith and in the power of God, unexperienced by you. Go forth in the strength of the God of Israel, and let your motto be: "The sword of the Lord and of Gideon." Judges 7: 18.

CHAPTER XXVI.

HEALING BY THE WORD.

Having been convinced that Jesus heals bodily infirmities now as in the days when He was here among men, and having received a desire to be healed, you should firmly believe the desire is from God, and go boldly to a throne of mercy to find grace to help in your time of great need. Should you at any time doubt as to whether your desire or knowledge is from God, you should try the spirit. If of God the spirit will "confess that Jesus Christ is come in the flesh," but if not of Him he will deny it. 1 John 4: 1-4; 1 Peter 4: 1, 2.

Those who have spiritual discrimination know that Satan does not always go dressed in his own garments; but sometimes comes as an angel of light, and unless tried as afore indicated, may deceive the very elect. Therefore, in whatever form he presents himself, you may be sure that his object is to deceive—never otherwise.

When God answers, in the desire, that He
will heal you, which He most asuredly
will (for if He had not intended to heal
you He never would have given you the
desire), your faith, received with the desire,
leaps into the promise, which, with the answer, God throws wide open, and in it is
your healing. Bless God, when He answers
you in the desire He not only unlocks the
promise, which was like a sealed up chest
full of useful tools, but gives it to you with
all its contents as your own property.

A desire is as worthless as an uncracked
nut in the hands of an infant, unless some-
one is found who is able and willing to
open it.

The thing desired is always inside of the
desire, as the kernel is in the nut, and to
get it out, you, like the child, must hand it
over to the author, who will open it and
give you its contents. God always has the
keys to His desires, and if presented to
Him will open every one of them and give
you their contents. Then I beseech you to
present them all to Him, as soon as received,
that He may unlock them and give you the
blessings they contain.

Having entered by grace through faith

into the promise, you must search out your
healing among the other gifts, all of which
God has graciously given you.   Here your
faith is no longer in the desire, but in the
promise in which you are to seek for the
healing until found, when you should take
it with a grip of steel, and hold on until
healed.

As soon as the healing is received by the
patient, and God says to the one with the gift
of healing (if present) to proceed, the healer
should in great faith and firmness say (if
the patient is possessed of devils): "Satan,"
or thou deaf, dumb or blind spirit (as the case
may be), "I command thee in the name of
Jesus Christ, the Son of the living God,
to come out of this body!"   Then having
cast out the evil spirit, let him lay hands on
the person being healed and say, "In the
name of Jesus of Nazareth, receive thy
healing," or sight or whatever is needed,
and steadfastly hold on by faith, and encour-
age the patient to hold on by faith until the
healing is complete; that is, until the power
of God (in the witness taken from the desire) enters the body, driving out the power
of Satan.   Then he should touch the healed
or lift him up (if fallen down under the

power of God), saying, "In the name of
the Lord Jesus, receive thy strength," or
such other words as the Holy Spirit may
give.

Taking your healing is like lifting the meat
out of the open nut and eating it. The nut
being cracked (or desire opened), your faith
enters into the shell (or desire), and according to the witness, which is knowledge
or power received to take your healing, you
lift the kernel, or thing desired, out of the
shell, or desire, and apply it where needed.
As you enter a burning house, drive out
the one who set it on fire, and put out the
fire, so the power in the witness, backed by
your taking-faith, all of and from God,
enters the afflicted body and drives out Satan, the author of sickness, and destroys the
disease.

When your healing is received, your taking-faith (received out of the desire) with
the witness or word of God (which is
knowledge or power) enters into the afflicted parts, and the power works according to your faith in healing the diseased
parts, the disease and enemy having been
cast out by the power of God. As the carpenter works in repairing a burned edifice,

so your faith backs the power of God in restoring the afflicted members to a normal condition.

Temptations will last until every fibre of the afflicted parts is healed. When the diseased members of the body are fully restored, Satan leaves off the temptations, and not before. When the carpenter works to repair, the Devil rages to prevent it. The Devil only roars when cast out, in order that he may get back. Therefore, fear not when temptations come on your soul or body work, for it is a sign you are on the right track, and Satan wants to drive you from it. For if you are on the wrong track, or not healed or saved, he is not going to bother you.

From this chapter we learn that the witness from within (given for your healing) is the word of God as revealed by the Holy Ghost; and in the witness or word is the power, and in the power is your healing. To take your healing from the word, by faith you take the witness, and in so doing you feel the power in the diseased part of the body, and your health comes forth out of the power felt in the body.

CHAPTER XXVII.

HEALING BY INSPIRATION.

On learning that you may be healed by inspiration—seeing your healing in the spirit before taking it into the body—and, having received a desire from God to thus have the cure performed, you should believe the desire to be from God and ask for faith to cover the disease, and hold on to God until He gives you the witness that your faith does cover it all in the spirit.

In seeking healing by inspiration you believe from the desire for faith to cover the disease first, instead, as in healing by the word, for the witness. In this you act like a wise man desiring to build a house, who in the beginning counts the cost, and secures ample means to complete it before commencing the work of building. The holding on is the trying of your faith until perfected, when you should commence using the tried faith or material, secured by your trial of faith for the edifice or healing in the spirit to be afterwards transferred from it to the body. As the wise man, on ascertaining that he has ample means, purchases the material and then goes to work to build the edifice, so you secure, by trials of your faith, a perfect faith, to believe for the witness and sight of your healing in the spirit before transferred to the body.

Having believed from the desire for faith you then believe in the faith for the witness and sight. Or, in other words, having first secured faith to cover the disease, you now ask (by the faith received out of the desire) for the witness or your healing in the spirit, which, when perfected, God gives you, and the sight or inspiration of your healing at the same time. Thus you see that God answers yes, to your petition, and with His promise gives you the sight of your healing in the spirit. Now you have three witnesses to your healing in the spirit—the desire, God's word (as revealed by the Holy Ghost), and your sight. The evidence is not only triple but intensified, inasmuch as knowledge is stronger than belief or desire. For in a desire, or the word, you feel for the promise by faith, without sight, while in the latter you see what you are promised before it is taken.

It is much easier to take a thing that is seen, when promised, than when not seen. For when seen, you know it exists and exactly where to reach for it when offered you; while, when not seen, you have only the donor's word without sight or knowledge as to its form or location in the desire, and have to go by faith from the promise and feeling in it until realized.

God always puts your healing and all other gifts to be taken from Him in a desire, whether taken from it direct or by His word or the embryo. In taking your healing into the body from the embryo seen in the spirit, you use a triple faith, the asking, taking, and overcoming-faith, which, combined, form a faith more than a hundred times stronger than the simple asking-faith, which most people are alone using to take God's blessings for soul and body.

Having received the desire, word, and sight of your healing, which is the inspiration of the word, and may be had in all God's gifts to man (*i. e.*, seen by our spiritual eyes before taken into our soul or body), it is an easy matter to lay hold through this triune or triple evidence, and transfer the healing from the spirit to the body.

The inspiration of healing in the spirit is like the inventor's mechanism before made. He has the inspiration of the invention before perfected, so that others can see it. It is the real table or chair in the spirit before made visible, and the inventor sees it, otherwise he would not have known what to make. So it is in the spirit; you see not as a vision or some imaginary thing as in speculation or spiritualism, but the embryo of the healing produced aftewards in the body.

When you see your healing in the spirit, you should take it with the overcoming-faith given with the sight or embryo, and transfer it to the body. In transferring the healing seen in the spirit by the united evidences of desire, hearing and sight, backed by the triune asking, taking and overcoming faith to the body, you use the fire and hammer of the word. The chain of evidences is now so complete, and the combined faith so perfect, that you drive your healing, seen in the spirit by the power of God, in your body with such force that the healing is complete and instantaneous.

In seeking your healing by inspiration you should remember that you believe, first, from the desire for the faith; second, in the faith for the witness and sight; third, trans- fer the healing seen in the spirit by your triune faith to the body. You should further remember that the embryo given you for your healing is a finished work of healing, done in the spirit before being done in the body; and, that in the embryo is the power, and in the power is your healing in the body. And that to take your healing from the embryo, you by faith, take the healing seen in the spirit, and by so doing you feel the power coming out of the embryo enter your body like sheet lightning, and from the power comes forth your healing.

If the healing is not received on these evidences you should, by trials of faith, per- fect the combined faith which gives chain- lightning power, and if not then taken you may go still further and take it on the impulse of the desire, word, and embryo, which is like forked lightning. Acts 2: 3.

In seeking healing you should use the method and degree needed to take it. In simple cases healing might be taken from the desire by simple asking-faith, or if more faith is needed, by a tried faith; or if still greater faith is needed, by an impulse on the desire. In more difficult cases you should take it from the witness, tried faith on it, or by impulse on the word. While in the most difficult cases you should take it from the embryo, tried faith on it, or by impulse on the sight in the spirit.

In summing up "the gifts of healing by the spirit of God," we learn there are at least three ways, and as many degrees to each way, making a total of nine gifts, or a trinity of trinities, by the same spirit. 1 Cor. 12: 9, 10.

CHAPTER XXVIII.

TRANCES.

A trance is a supernatural state of body and mind. Dr. Doddridge defines it as, "Such a rapture of mind as gives the person who falls into it a look of astonishment, and renders him insensible of the external objects around him, while in the meantime his imagination is agitated in an extraordinary manner with some striking scenes which

pass before it and take up all the attention."
Stockius describes it as, "A sacred ecstacy
or rapture of the mind out of itself, when,
the use of the external senses being sus-
pended, God reveals something in a pecu-
liar manner to prophets and apostles, who
are then taken or transported out of themselves."*

"The same idea is intimated in the Eng-
lish word Trance, from the Latin, *transitus*,
the state of being carried out of one's self."
—McClintock and Strong's Bib. Cyclo-
pædia.

The reader should bear in mind that one
must be in a trance in order to see a vision.
Therefore it follows that where there is a
spiritual vision, there is also a trance,
though it may not be so worded.

Balaam fell, "into a trance but having his
eyes open." Numb. 24: 4.

Isaiah was in a trance when he had that
vision of the Lord. Isa. 6: 1-13.

Ezekiel was in a trance when he saw a
great vision of the idolatry of Jerusalem.
Ezek., chapters 8, 9, 10, 11. He was also

---

*(This definition is defective in this, that the author con-
fines trances to prophets and apostles.)

in a trance when he saw the vision of dry bones. Ezek. 37.

Daniel was in a trance when he saw the scenes described in chapters 7, 8, 9, 10.

Peter was in a trance when he saw "a certain vessel descending unto him," from the heavens. Act. 10: 10-12.

Paul fell into a trance while he was praying in Jerusalem. Acts. 22: 17, 18. He was also in a trance when he was "caught up into paradise." 2 Cor. 12: 1-5.

John was in a trance when he saw the wonderful scenes described in the book of Revelation; all of which please read with care.

God desires His children to stand up and honor the Holy Ghost. Many have the form of godliness but deny the power. Arise and shine in God's will. Will you do it?

The Holy Ghost is a wonderful person. At times He is very noisy, and at all times when His leadings are followed, signs and wonders follow. Especially in these last days we may expect them.

In olden times holy men of God spake as they were moved by the Holy Ghost. Peter, in defending his Master's cause on the day of Pentecost, told them that the signs and wonders seen were for them and their children, which reaches down to us and now. There are few such men as Peter in these days.

Many run from God. They are afraid when the Holy Ghost comes as He often does in meetings. Some of these have no doubt crossed the death-line and are damned. Let us honor the Holy Ghost. Are you going down to hell? Stop! He who honors the Holy Ghost honors God and has life.

Jesus pronounced a fearful doom on favored Capernaum. O, ye ministers of God, preach the pure and whole Gospel. Jesus did, and was crucified. So it may be with you. Paul preached the truth. He didn't get up a school-boy's essay and read it off as many D. D.'s are doing to-day.

Paul had to be knocked down before he could see the turpitude of his sin. Afterwards he had many visions or trances. Pray more and you will see more of them. O, ye stiffnecked and uncircumcised in heart and ears, be careful lest ye fight against God.

Paul was a wonderful man. At one time

he was caught up to the third heaven. O,
the vision he then had! It was so grand
thst he forgot whether he was in or out of
the body.

A trance is simply to be overpowered by
the power of God. The overcoming power
is of the Holy Ghost. Man's power is
swallowed up by the power of God. All
the displays of the Holy Ghost, whether in
shouts, prayer or trances, are of God.

John was carried away by the Spirit in
many trances or visions, in which he saw
Jesus, heaven, the angels, and the blood-
washed throng singing redemption songs.
About all we know of heaven has been
revealed through trances. Peter had a
trance immediately before God called him
to go and preach to Cornelius. Stephen
lost his life for telling what he saw in a
trance.

The greatest opposition Jesus and His
Apostles had, came from the doctors of the
law. They falsely accused them, and like
blood-hounds hunted them down to death.
Stephen's face shone in the midst of these
doctors like the face of an angel. So we
may shine, in some degree, as did Jesus on
the mount of transfiguration, or as Moses,

while talking to the Israelites after his forty
days' walk with God in the holy mountain.
O, thou eternal God, put the shine on us
just now, for Jesus' sake! Hallelujah!

You must be in a trance to see a vision.
The natural eyes can not see God; but in a
trance you see through your soul's eyes, and
may see Him, for your eyes are then His
eyes, and not your own.

Isaiah was in a trance. He was called of
God, but not prepared, so God showed him
in a vision, his heart, and how to get it
cleansed from all sin. He got down and let
God sanctify him. O, let us get down at
the feet of Jesus and be cleansed from all sin.
The live coal represented the anointing and
cleansing of the Holy Ghost. Isaiah was
then ready to go; he had no excuse. Hear
him exclaim: "Here am I; send me!"

He who has been called of God to preach
the Gospel, and has ceased to do so, is to be
pitied. When one is called, it is for life.
Daniel was often in trances. His profes-
sional friends ran away from him, but the
Lord called him His greatly beloved and
told him what to do.

One of the old saints lay in a trance for
three days. Ezekiel, in a vision, saw the

church as a valley of dry bones. At one time
he was carried away in a vision by God, by
the hair of his head, and let down at Jerusalem. God may have to thus carry some of
us about in these days in order to convince
us that He is God.

In olden times the people were not afraid
to hold up holy hands and with a loud voice
say, "Amen, amen, amen," and bow their
faces to the ground. God help the people
to get the starch out of their worship so
they can shout with a great shout, "Glory to
God! I am saved!" In olden times Christians used to praise the Lord for themselves,
but now many church members want to
hire some one else to do it for them.

Let us encircle the walls of Jericho the
seventh time, and with a shout see the walls
tumble to the ground; or, as in the days of
Gideon, break the pitchers and see God
conquer the enemy without bloodshed. O,
the faith required to conquer the world for
Jesus!

In that most wonderful meeting just held
by the Trance Evangelist, Mrs. M. B.
Woodworth, in Indianapolis, about one
thousand persons were saved, several hundred healed of all kinds of diseases, and

from one to ten in a trance at almost every
meeting, one of whom remained in that
state seventeen hours. Some of them
when in a trance had visions of the indes-
cribable horrors of hell, with Satan riding
on a black horse of death, with spear in
hand to strike down all who opposed him.
Others saw heaven, the beautiful gates, the
gold-paved streets, and some of their
friends. Others saw the Savior with His
pierced side and the prints of the nails in
His hands and feet.

The Trance Evangelist says: "When
called to preach my voice was very weak.
The Lord gives me a voice as I need it. At
first I could not carry a tune, but now at
times I can be heard a mile. My voice at
times seems to come from my lips. It is a
special gift from God.

"Since my anointing, which was brought
about through the teaching of some
Friends, the trances came on. The anointing was like a cloud of glory. At times it
seems as though I could fly. The anointing abideth. It is power, and controlled
me even before I had what the world calls
trances.

"Oh, it is wonderful how God works!

We simply put ourselves in His hands and He uses us. What He gives we joyfully use to save the people. We never yet had a house large enough to hold the people. When we have trances people are shown us hanging over the pit of hell, and such need to repent speedily or they are lost."

The author first attended Sister Woodworth's meetings in June, 1885, at Kokomo, Ind., and saw the power of God wonderfully manifested in the conversion of sinners, in the anointing of believers and in trances.

The house would seat about four thousand, and was filled nearly all the time, and at times crowds were unable to gain admittance. In her short stay of three weeks, there were about 500 converted, 100 baptized and twenty-five in trances.

In the spring of 1885 it pleased the Lord to have some of his children start a faith-meeting in Chicago, Ill., where a great many were healed of all manner of diseases. When children of the same family are all born again, they may draw living water from the same fountain, and be healed of all manner of diseases as when Jesus of Nazareth was on earth.

The most wonderful demonstration of power seen during the meetings was near midnight on the 2d of July, 1885, when nearly forty persons lay where they had fallen when healed, waiting for strength to arise and shine for Jesus. It took till daylight to clear the room of those healed, so powerful did the Holy Ghost fall upon the people. But glory to God, they all went away healed. Could you see the many crutches left at these meetings you would say: "These signs shall follow them that believe." Mark 16: 17. Praise the Lord!

While at Chicago the author saw in those gospel faith-meetings in two nights over fifty people fall entranced, (if you prefer the term), under the raining bullets of the Holy Ghost, and scores converted and healed of all manner of diseases.

It was here we first saw the people fall in great numbers, in answer to our prayer and laying on of hands in faith meetings. Indeed, several times we came very near going down under the mighty power of the Lord.

During the summer of 1886 we preached twenty-seven times in Louisville, Ky. From one to twenty-five fell at each meeting,

under the power of the Holy Ghost.   Some
of them remained in an unconscious state
for hours.   Seek God's power, if you would
see His glory.